"It'll be pretty this morning with the new snow," I said. Mom looked wiped out, and I wanted to say something else to cheer her up. "Mom, remember last night? That was fun, and you looked great in that red dress."

For an instant, her face was blank, as if she was thinking, Last night? Red dress? Then a little smile appeared. "Yeah, it was. Sort of stupid fun. I should have let you sleep."

"No, I'm glad you woke me up." I glanced at the clock. "I have to go; the bus'll be coming."

She pointed to her cheek. "Plant me one right here. Come on, you're not too big to kiss your mother." The same thing she always said. She held me around the waist, and I bent and kissed her. "I love you, honey," she said.

"Love you, too." It was automatic. That's what I can't forget.

Also by
NORMA FOX MAZER

AFTER THE RAIN

BABYFACE

CRAZY FISH

DOWNTOWN

GOODNIGHT, MAMAN

MISSING PIECES

OUT OF CONTROL

SILVER

TAKING TERRI MUELLER

WHEN SHE WAS GOOD

NORMA FOX MAZER

girlhearts

HarperTrophy®
An Imprint of HarperCollins*Publishers*

My thanks to Dr. James Greenwald
and to Barbara Wright,
both of whom generously gave me their time
and helped me with information.

Harper Trophy® is a registered trademark of HarperCollins Publishers Inc.

Girlhearts
Copyright © 2001 by Norma Fox Mazer
For permission to reprint a portion of the poem "On Second Thought" by Meg
Kearney on page ix, we gratefully acknowledge the author. From *An Unkindness of
Raisins*, BOA Editions, 2001.
All rights reserved. No part of this book may be used or reproduced in any manner
whatsoever without written permission except in the case of brief quotations embod-
ied in critical articles and reviews. Printed in the United States of America. For
information address HarperCollins Children's Books, a division of HarperCollins
Publishers, 1350 Avenue of the Americas, New York, NY 10019.

Library of Congress Cataloging-in-Publication Data
Mazer, Norma Fox, date.
   Girlhearts/Norma Fox Mazer.
      p.   cm.
   Summary: Thirteen-year-old Sarabeth Silver's life is turned upside down when her
mother dies suddenly, leaving her orphaned, confused, and at the mercy of everyone
who seems to know what is best for her.
   ISBN 0-688-13350-9—ISBN 0-688-06866-9 (lib. bdg.)
   ISBN 0-380-72290-9 (pbk.)
   [1. Grief—Fiction.   2. Orphans—Fiction.   3. Death—Fiction.   4. Mothers
and daughters—Fiction.   5. Family problems—Fiction.]   I. Title.
PZ7.M47398 Gi   2001   00-063202
[Fic]—dc21   CIP
                                                                          AC

Typography by Andrea Vandergrift
❖
First Harper Trophy edition, 2002

Visit us on the World Wide Web!
www.harperteen.com

girlhearts

ON SECOND THOUGHT

I was wrong about happiness. I thought
if I just knew where to look it would be
easily retrievable, like a hair brush
I lost between the cushions of the couch,
or the name of someone I used to know.

—Meg Kearney

1

On the last night of my mother's life, she came into my room in the middle of the night and called my name. I was dreaming, and her voice became mixed with the dream. A big green bird was talking to me. How intelligent, I thought, and then I woke up. My room was dim, only a little light filtering in around the edges of the shades, and there was Mom standing by my bed, saying, "Sarabeth, come on, wake up."

"What time is it?" I said.

"Two o'clock, I think." She took me by the shoulders. "Come on, sweetie, up. You have to see this."

As mysterious as her words was the way she was dressed, as if for a party, in a close-fitting red dress with a deep neckline. It had been hanging in her closet for years.

"You look nice," I said. "What's happening?"

She handed me my clothes. "You'll see."

She took my hand and pulled me through

the house, out the door, and down our road. The air was chilly and had that wet earth smell of late fall. Everything was dark, dark and quiet. Not even a dog barked.

At the top of the long blacktop road that wound down the hill, Mom stopped. "It's not there! Where is it?"

I wondered if something awful was happening to her, the way it had to Melissa Schmid's mother. Everyone in school had heard about Mrs. Schmid running down her street naked, calling out for eyeglass donations. "For protection, for protection, people, do you hear me?" she was shouting when the ambulance came.

"Mom." I moved closer to her. "Are you okay?"

She seized my hand again, and we ran down the hill toward the highway. A wind came up and blew against our faces. "Yes," Mom whispered. She pointed across the road. On one side, our side, the pavement was dry; on the other side, rain drizzled down in a soft silvery sheet. The split between the two sides was as neat as if someone had laid it out with a ruler.

"Cool," I said.

Mom gave me a triumphant smile. "Was that worth getting up for or what? I couldn't sleep," she said, wrapping her arms around herself, "so I got dressed and went out for a walk. I was just walking around, all around, and then I saw this, and—"

"Why couldn't you sleep?"

"—I heard the rain on the pavement, you know that sound, sort of pattering? I could smell it! I love that smell. Then I saw this, this *curtain* of rain, only it was happening higher up, at the top of the road, where we stopped before, and it was so . . . beautiful. So beautiful. I just had to show you."

She was still wearing only the red dress, not even a sweater over it, and it seemed to me that she glowed, as if lit from within by a secret fire. "So beautiful," she said again. "Beautiful and mysterious. What do you think it means? Do you think it means something? Maybe it means my luck will change."

I stepped across to the other side of the road and stood in the drizzle. "Maybe it's a sign from the universe," I said, and I wished I'd thought of something more original.

"I could use a sign from the universe." Mom moved her hands as if parting the curtain of rain and came to stand next to me. "A sign from anywhere, actually. Hey, universe," she yelled.

"Shhh, Mom!" The rain was coming down harder. We were both getting wet. "We should go back," I said. "We're wet as noodles."

"Yeah." But suddenly she covered her face, her shoulders shook, and little mewling sounds came out from between the fence of her fingers. Was she laughing or crying? Was it the Leo thing again?

Leo had a new girlfriend, a woman with the ridiculous name of Pepper Black. Mom insisted it didn't bother her, that she was glad for him. She had been the one to make the break happen, she reminded me. "I should have done it a long time ago. Leo's sweet, and I'll never stop loving him, but we were a worn-out story."

She said the same thing to Cynthia Ramos, her best friend, and she even talked about it to some of our neighbors, but in the past week or so, her mood had changed. Two nights ago, she'd had a real crying jag. It was strange. She never cried.

"Mom," I said, touching her bent head. I didn't want her to cry and feel rotten. And I didn't want to hear her crying and feel rotten myself. "Let's go, Mom."

She parted her hands, looking out at me. "First, we drink rain."

"Mom," I protested.

"Honey, this is special. Sign from the universe, remember? We drink rain for luck. Good luck, that is. Do I need good luck? Yes. Do you need good luck? Yes. Everybody needs good luck." She lifted her face, and now she was laughing, definitely laughing. "Come on, Sarabeth. You, too. Drink the rain!"

"Mom . . ."

"Is that all you can say? Maaoom," she bleated.

I pulled my hair in a wet bunch over my shoulder. My mother was unlike anyone else's. Harder working, younger, prettier, poorer, and, I thought with a tiny pang of guilt, weirder. I opened my mouth and drank rain.

2

When I walked into the kitchen, Mom was standing with her back to the sink, gripping a cup of coffee. No red dress this morning, just work clothes—jeans and a plaid shirt. The rain had turned to snow, and Mom's mood had turned, too, though I didn't realize it at first.

"Cup number which?" I said. I turned the radio up a notch. They were playing a song I liked. "I know that's not your first cup." I'd been trying to get her to cut down on the coffee drinking.

"Three . . . I guess." She frowned into the cup. "Might be four."

"Mom!" Tobias was curled up in his favorite place, near the refrigerator, wheezing away. He had a cold. I nudged him over with my foot and took out the milk carton. Mom had already put the cornflakes box and a bowl and spoon on the table for me. "You said you were going to cut back to two cups, max, in the morning."

She gave a shudder and gestured at the window

over the sink. "It's snowing out there. Snow already, and it's only the middle of November. This is a bad omen. What are we going to have this winter, fifteen feet of snow for the car to break down in every day?"

"We got through last winter okay," I said.

"That's not the way I remember it."

I sat down and poured cornflakes into the bowl. The heater was going full blast in the other room, but chilly air rippled around my legs. We were never completely warm after summer.

The news came on. Mom yanked the radio plug out of the socket. The off-on knob had been missing forever. "What are we listening to this junk for? Same old, same old, bad music and worse news." Then, without missing a beat, she started on me. "Sarabeth, look at you. Your posture is awful. Is that the way you're going to school? Your jeans are torn! And that shirt— ugh, it's way too bright and *way* too tight."

I looked down at myself. Tight? So what? I had nothing to show, not like Mom. She had the real thing. You could see her breasts even under her loose plaid shirt.

"Go and change, right now," she said. She

started rummaging around in the tote bag she carried to work with her. "Where's my scarf? Have you seen my fish scarf?"

"Are you thinking about Leo, Mom?" That could explain her big mood plunge. Leo had been almost the best thing in our lives, right up there with Cynthia and Billy. We'd as good as lost them, too, when they moved over to the north side of the city.

"What's the color of that shirt, anyway?" Mom said.

I tucked my feet up on the chair rung. "Violet."

"It's vio*lent*."

"My friends like this shirt."

"Oh, your friends." One of her cheeks was streaked red, as if someone had smeared crayon over it. Veins or something.

"What does that mean, Mom?" She'd always liked my friends.

"It means bad taste, Sarabeth. Your friends and you. And don't you dare say you got that from me."

Laugh line, I guess, but I didn't feel like congratulating her with even a snicker. Had I dreamed last night, the two of us getting wet together, then dashing back through the rain, holding hands and, once inside, drying each other's heads?

At that moment, I remembered my actual dream, the one with the green bird, and I realized that the bird had been James. James from the bus. James from my algebra class. James! Wrong shape, wrong color, but James, and he'd talked to me.

"Why do you have that look on your face?" Mom said.

"What look? Why do you have that look on *your* face?"

"Don't be a freshmouth!"

"I'm not. Don't call me that, Mom."

She held the coffee cup next to her cheek. "You think it's so terrible? That's what my mother used to say. 'Freshmouth. You're a freshmouth, Jane Halley.'"

"And what did you say?"

"It doesn't matter." Which meant, Subject closed.

I didn't know Mom's parents or my father's or, for that matter, any of my relatives. All I knew was that they had all lived in a town called Hinchville and when Mom got pregnant, no one helped her and my father, even though they were just teenagers, neither one even out of school yet.

"Are we quarreling this morning?" Mom sat down and scooted her chair close to mine. "Let's not." She took me by the chin. Her hands were chilly. "Look at that face. I love that face. You're so pretty, Sarabeth. But sloppy. I want you to be proud of yourself."

"Mom, come on, I have to eat." I knew where she was headed, right to the "Rules for Life" lecture. After "Be proud of yourself" came "Study hard," then "Go to college," and "Don't get involved with boys," and "No sex until you're through school." Et cetera.

"Look at the clock," I said. "Time to go!" I got up and put my dish in the sink.

The phone rang. I reached too fast for the receiver, and the base fell off the knob on the wall and crashed to the floor. "Sorry about that," I said, picking up the base.

"Say 'Silver residence,'" Mom hissed.

I made a face at her, but I said it. "Silver residence."

"This is Mrs. Milleritz. Is that Sarabeth?"

"Yes, it is, Mrs. Milleritz."

"Dear, will you tell your mother I don't need her to clean today? Today is her day to come to me, but tell her not today."

"Okay, Mrs. Milleritz."

"Tell her next week as usual, but not today. Thank you much, dear. Don't forget," she trilled, "not today, next week."

"Alison Milleritz is canceling again?" Mom said, when I hung up. "She's always canceling, and then calling and changing her mind, just when I'm going to someone else. She's impossible." She slumped over the table, her head on her arms.

"Mom, she said she wants you as usual next week."

"Yeah, yeah," she said into her arms.

"Is this going to screw up our budget?"

"Yeah, yeah."

"I feel like calling her back," I said. "I want to tell her off. I want to tell her how miserable she is to you."

"No, no!" She sat up, looking alarmed. "Don't do that!"

"Mom, I wouldn't do it. I just said I felt like doing it."

She nodded and pressed her fingers into her forehead. "Oh, Lord, I'm so tired." She reached for the phone, dialed, and said in a bright, punched-up voice that I hated, "Mrs. Reigel? Hi. This is Jane Silver. I have a free day today, and I remember you said you needed some extra help. . . . No, no . . . of course . . . sure . . . the usual . . . G'bye to you, too."

She dialed again. "Mr. Alberts? Hi, how are you? Jane Silver here. I'm free today if you'd like me to come over and take care of the attic? You were saying you wanted it cleaned. . . ."

I left. I didn't want to hear any more. I changed my jeans and brushed my teeth. "Any luck?" I said when I came back. I knelt and petted Tobias. His poor eyes were crusted, and his fur was dry.

Mom shook her head. "Maybe I'll just sleep today"—she looked out the window—"or maybe I'll go for a walk over in the park first."

"It'll be pretty this morning with the new

snow," I said. Mom looked wiped out, and I wanted to say something else to cheer her up. "Mom, remember last night? That was fun, and you looked great in that red dress."

For an instant, her face was blank, as if she was thinking, Last night? Red dress? Then a little smile appeared. "Yeah, it was. Sort of stupid fun. I should have let you sleep."

"No, I'm glad you woke me up." I glanced at the clock. "I have to go; the bus'll be coming."

She pointed to her cheek. "Plant me one right here. Come on, you're not too big to kiss your mother." The same thing she always said. She held me around the waist, and I bent and kissed her. "I love you, honey," she said.

"Love you, too." It was automatic. That's what I can't forget.

3

"Hello! What's your name?" A boy with blond hair sat down next to me on the school bus.

"Sarabeth. What's yours?"

"Sam." He held out his hand for me to shake. He was about nine years old. I'd seen him on the bus before, but this was the first time we'd talked. He started telling me about a show he'd seen the night before, some *Star Trek* thing.

"Uh-huh, uh-huh," I said, yawning and leaning on my hand. I was probably the only person left in the universe who was a complete *Star Trek* idiot. Now and then, Mom tried to bring me up to par. I had gotten a little interested when she told me that my father, Benjamin Robert Silver— which was the way she talked about him sometimes, almost as if he had been a movie star or someone fabulous she had once known—had been a Trekkie, but even that hadn't taken.

Sam talked without stopping for at least fifteen minutes. All *Star Trek* stuff. I could easily have fallen asleep to the sound of his voice. "So what do you think?" he said finally.

I sat up. "What do I think about what?"

"What I just said. The whole story I told you. Duuuh! Did you like it?"

"Mmm," I said.

"Were you listening?" he asked suspiciously.

"Sure," I said.

The bus stopped just then at City Heights, which was full of the kind of houses Mom cleaned. Huge, with multiple chimneys and rows of big shiny windows and four-car garages. Then James got on and, when I saw him, the bird dream came winging back to me.

"You glad I told you the story, anyway?" Sam said.

"What? Oh . . . yes . . . sure."

James walked by me. I could have reached out and touched his arm. I glanced at him and then away, as if I wasn't interested. He had really big ears, like that basketball player who was so cute, but whose ears stuck out like satellite dishes.

"You didn't say thanks," Sam said.

"For what, the story? Okay, thanks."

15

"You're welcome." He looked at me as if he wasn't a foot shorter and six years younger. "You're pretty."

"Are you hitting on me, or do you mean pretty old?"

I turned my head a fraction again and saw James across the aisle and three rows back. There was an empty seat behind him. If I had the nerve, I could get up and sit down there, the way Sam had sat down next to me. I'd lean over the seat and tell him my dream, and maybe I'd even tell him about Mom and me running through the rain.

"Sarabeth! You want to hear another *Star Trek* story?" Sam pulled at my sleeve.

"Sam! Want the truth? No, I don't. We don't have the time for it anyway." The bus was pulling into the school parking lot. "Boo hoo, too bad, so sad," I added.

"Mean person," he said.

"Am I?" I stood and pulled on my backpack. "I hope not. I was just teasing." All the time, I was watching James from the corner of my eye, checking out who he was talking to.

"Maybe you *are* mean," Sam said. "And maybe

16

you're not." He shrugged. "How could I know? It's up to you."

"Aren't you the wise old man!" I tapped him on the shoulder and we got off the bus. I could sense James walking in the crowd behind me, but I didn't turn around again.

"Oh, girl," Patty sang into the wet, snowy air, "your heart is pure and strong. . . . You know the way I love you . . ." The warmth of the words, the coolness of her perfect face, that was Patty, through and through. ". . . and though I've sometimes done you wrong," she sang, her arms linked with Asa's and Jennifer's, "I'm begging you . . . listen to me now, girl. . . . Don't make us part."

The words shook me. It was Patty's voice, the feeling in it. She could look and sound remote, but after last year, I knew just how strong she was, just how emotional.

"Girlheart, girlheart," Jennifer and I joined in on the chorus.

It was after school, and the four of us were on the way to the mall. I gestured to Asa, Come on, you sing, too, but she shook her head and made the puking motion. Unsentimental Asa!

"All I need is for you to say," Jennifer, Patty, and I sang, "you'll let me into your girlheart, today."

We held onto the last note: ". . . aaaaaaaaay." Patty gave out first, and then I did, but Jennifer, who was a runner and had the lungs for it, stayed on it. "What a song, what a song!" she said when she finally let go of the note.

"I don't know how you can all fall for that stuff," Asa said. "Those lyrics are so manipulative. 'Let me into your heart. . . . I know I've done wrong,' bla, bla, bla, whine, whine, whine."

Asa spoke just the way she looked—decisive, firm, solid. Patty said that Asa had always had that deep voice, even when she was a little kid, as if she'd always been on the way to her future, which, we all predicted, was to be a judge, like her father.

"That guy in the song is not really sorry," she went on; "he's just trying to get in good with her again."

"How do you know it's a guy who's saying it?" Jennifer said.

"Jen! It's obvious."

"I don't think it's so obvious. It could be two girls in love, and one of them——"

"You're just being outrageous, and exorbitantly so," Asa said.

"Exorbitantly so? Excuse me? Could you try talking like a regular human being?"

"Could you try expanding your vocabulary?"

I only half listened. All day, I'd felt distracted, slightly off balance. Maybe I was getting sick, like Grant, who'd been home with the flu all week. Anyway, Jen and Asa were always bickering; it was nothing new. Maybe they did a little less of it when Grant was with us. She was a calming influence on everyone.

"Asa, did I tell you I like your braids," Patty said.

"Changing the subject, Patty?" Jennifer asked.

Asa tossed her head, making her African-style braids with beads clink. "It took forever to get them done, but it was worth it."

"Negative, negative," Jennifer crowed. "I'm surprised at you, Asa, the big liberal, taking over someone else's culture. Braids on Diane McArdle and the other African-American girls are cool, but on you—"

"I know the argument," Asa interrupted, "and I don't accept it. If you wear an embroidered blouse, are you stealing my Armenian culture? If I wear overalls"—which she did nearly every day of the week—"am I stealing a farmer's culture? If a guy has a beard," she steamrollered on, "is he stealing Sarabeth's father's Jewish culture?"

"Your father was Jewish, Silver?" Jennifer asked. She was the only one still calling me that. Over the summer, Patty, Asa, and Grant had all started calling me Sarabeth. Just as I'd been glad when they dubbed me Silver, now I was glad they'd dropped it. It made me more part of the group; not the only one with a nickname.

I nodded. "But no beard."

"Wow, I didn't know you were, too," Jennifer said.

"Were, too, what?"

"Jewish, like me. Oh, wait, is your mother?"

"What, Jewish? No."

"Too bad! Then you aren't, either."

We stopped on the corner of Erie Boulevard, waiting for the light to change. The sky was heavy, a color like dulled silver, which probably meant more snow. Cars passed in a stream of noise and fumes.

"Your mother has to be Jewish for you to be,"

Jennifer said, hooking her arm through mine. "That's our law. But it's cool that your father was; it sort of connects you and me more."

"I'm not through with what I wanted to say about my braids," Asa said. "Jen, is your criticism of my hairdo about culture or envy?" She gave Jennifer's frizzy red hair a hard tug.

Jennifer liked that. She liked anything physical. She laughed and dashed across the four lanes ahead of us.

In the mall, we wandered, looking at clothes and makeup. After a while, we went upstairs to the food court. "I'll keep the table warm while you all go get some food," I said, putting my jacket over the back of a chair.

"Are you on a diet, Sarabeth?" Asa said. She hooked her thumbs through her overall straps. "You better not be! You're skinny enough."

"Jennifer's skinnier," I said.

"Jen's all muscle. You're not in her class, Sarabeth. You cannot afford to lose one more ounce."

"Judge Asa has proclaimed," Jennifer said, throwing off her jacket.

"I just don't want anything, Asa. I'm not

21

hungry." I sat down, hooking my heels on the chair rung.

What I didn't say, and what I wouldn't say, was that Mrs. Milleritz's call that morning was almost a guarantee that Mom would be short of cash by the end of the month and maxing out her credit card to pay bills. She'd be fishing around for every spare quarter. The few dollars I'd spend now might not look like much to my friends, but they were big to Mom and me.

I watched Jennifer, Asa, and Patty walking over to the food court. At the Chinese place, Jennifer turned and made an "are you sure?" face at me. I nodded and waved her on. Jennifer liked to annoy people for the sheer hell of it, but she was good. I really loved her, loved them all, everything about them. Even their names seemed special to me. Patty Lewis. Asa Goronkian. Jennifer Rosen. Grant Varrow.

The four of them had been friends forever. I was the newbie. Well, not completely. It was over a year now since I'd been new in school and they'd taken me into their group. Since September, James was new in school, too, and new on the school bus, which he didn't take regularly, but just often enough to feed my crush.

When Patty, Jennifer, and Asa came back, they had pizzas and sodas. Jennifer put a can of soda down in front of me. "Jen, I don't want anything," I said.

"Too bad, it's for you, and I'm not taking it back."

I reached into my jeans and pushed a bill across the table to her. Jen pushed it back. "Hello! It's a present; you can thank me."

"Thank you, but I can pay." I pushed the money toward her again. Back it came. "Jen!"

"Silver!" she mimicked. She picked up a slice. "Drink up. You don't always have to be so freakin' independent."

"My stepfather bought a Lexus," Patty said. "Okay if we talk about that, you two? He said he needed it for his law practice. Did I tell you all this already? He took my college money to pay for it."

"No, you didn't tell us. He took your college money?" Asa froze with a slice halfway to her mouth. "He can't do that."

"He did it," Patty said. "The account was in Mom's name, and when they got married, she

23

made everything joint with him."

"What a venal, awful man," Asa said. "That is so bad. That's wicked and greedy." Her nose pointed forward in outrage. "And your mother, what's the matter with her, Patty? Why did she just give him the account?"

"Same reason she married him. She's in luuuve. He is, too. With himself." Waves of color passed over Patty's pale cheeks.

Patty's and my bad joke together was that both our mothers had been busy over the summer, Patty's acquiring husband Kevin in July and mine disposing of boyfriend Leo in August.

"The more I live with him, the less I know how my mother could have fallen for him," Patty said. "Sometimes, I wish I could just get out of there."

I moved my chair closer to hers. "If it gets too bad, Patty, you can always come live with us again."

She nodded. "I might take you up on that, I really might."

"Negative, negative," Jennifer said, bouncing in her seat. "No more moves, Patty! You've moved around too much already. It's not good for you.

First, you left your uncle's house, which, okay, I know you had to, but still, it was a move. Then you went to live with Sarabeth, where you were all crowded and crammed together, and then you and your mom got that apartment on Oak Street, which was no big deal, let's admit it, and *now*— now, at least, you've got a house of your own—"

"I don't look at it as mine, actually," Patty said.

"—and a room of your own," Jennifer went on, "a nice room, and if you moved in with Silver—well, why would you do it? What for, what would you gain? You'd be living all squeezed up—"

"'All crowded and crammed,'" I put in. "Our place isn't that small, Jen."

"Hey, it's a trailer." Jennifer gave my arm one of her trademark squeezes. I'd have a black-and-blue mark tomorrow. "Don't go getting all sensitive on me, Silver."

When we left the food court, I stopped at the phone booth near the outside door to call Mom. I got our answering machine and Mom's message. "Hello, we're all busy right now. Leave a message, and someone or other will return your call." She always tried to make it sound like there were more people than just the two of us living there.

"Hey, Mom," I said, "you there? Hello, hello. You want to pick up? Okay, I guess you're not there. I'm going out for the bus now. I'll be home in half an hour."

Outside, we waited under the Plexiglas shelter. People poured out of the mall, hurrying to their cars in the lot. Patty and Jennifer's bus pulled up, steaming and heaving. A few minutes later, Asa's bus stopped. I was alone in the shelter. It was snowing again, big wet flakes that probably wouldn't last too long. Cars went by on the boulevard with their lights on, and the sky got darker and darker.

4

It was past five when I got home. I went around turning on lights. Tobias was sleeping again near the refrigerator. "You don't feel any better?" I asked him, kneeling down to pet him. "Where's Mom? She should be home by now."

I put a tape Grant had lent me in the cassette player, and checked the fridge to see if Mom had left a note about supper. No. What she had left, though, was her good old black shoulder bag, the one she took everywhere, the one that was stuffed with everything she needed when she went to work. It was lying on the counter, half-open, and when I looked inside, I saw that her wallet was there, along with all the other junk she toted. For a moment, I zipped and unzipped the bag, trying to figure out why Mom had gone off in the car without wallet, license, or money.

Maybe, after I'd left, someone had called her to work, and she'd just grabbed the car keys and run out. That would explain the breakfast dishes still in the sink and her bed still unmade. Mom never went out and left her bed unmade. But still, she should have been home by now.

Okay, say she went to work, came home, and decided to go out again, and *this* was when she grabbed the car keys and forgot her shoulder bag. But where would she be going with just car keys and nothing else? To see Cynthia, of course. "Duuuh," I said out loud, and picked up the phone.

Cynthia answered on the first ring. "It's me," I said. "Let me speak to Mom, please."

"Jane's not here, Sarabeth. It's just me and the baby. Was she planning to come over?"

"I don't know. I just thought . . . Cynthia, she isn't home yet."

"So?"

I paused. "So, nothing. Except, she should be home."

"Oh . . . my." Cynthia was laughing at me. "You two are so attached. At the hip, I swear. What are you worried about? Maybe she had some errands to do."

"Yeah, that's actually what I was thinking." Little white lie, but better than having Cynthia laugh at me again.

After I hung up, I peeled potatoes, made burger patties, and put a pot of water on the stove to heat. I kept watching the clock. I made a salad, set the table, and sliced the potatoes straight into the boiling water, a habit that drove Mom up the wall.

Around 6:30, I went to the front door and looked out. Lights were on all around in the court. The snow had stopped, and the sky was clearing. Big drifts of fat clouds passed overhead. There was a little slice of moon showing in the sky on the other side of the highway.

By seven, I was too hungry to wait for Mom any longer. I mashed the potatoes and threw a burger on the pan. When I finished eating and Mom still wasn't home, I started calling my friends. Grant first. She had her own phone with her own phone number and had probably never peeled a potato in her life. "Do you know how to peel potatoes?" I asked.

"Is that a special skill?" Grant said hoarsely.

"Yeah, you go to potato-peeling school. Do you feel better?"

"Better than yesterday," she croaked, "but my throat is still sore. I stayed in bed practically the whole day. I didn't mind, though. I listened to music for hours."

Grant had changed my ideas forever about rich girls. She was the calmest and the most unspoiled person I knew, even if she didn't know how to peel potatoes. By the time we stopped talking, it was past eight. I made cocoa and watched TV for a while. At 8:30, I called Cynthia again. "Did I tell you that Mom went out without her shoulder bag?"

"Okay. So?"

"Don't you think that's a little strange?"

"Not really. I forget things all the time. Are you panicking because she's late getting home? Cut the woman a little slack, Sarabeth; she's a big girl. Let her out of your pocket."

"I'm not panicking, Cynthia, and I don't have Mom in my pocket. Whatever that means."

"She'll probably walk in the door the minute you hang up."

"Right," I said.

I hung up. Mom didn't walk in the door.

I went in her room and turned on the computer. One of the women she cleaned for, a lawyer, had given it to Mom a few months ago, when she bought a new one for herself. Nothing wrong with it; it was just a little old, a little slow, but we loved it.

I found Asa on-line. "wsup?" she asked.

"not mch. my mom's not home yet. i called cynthia & she really annoyed me. she sd don't panik, like i panik all the time."

"cyn ust 2b yr momz best frend?" Asa asked.

"so rite. they moved away, closer 2 the army base."

"hez a soljer?"

"u got it."

"yuk."

"they hav a kid now, darren."

"cute?"

"spoiled."

"ha! lol!"

Then we talked about Grant and, after that, about Patty's stepfather, Kevin, and how much Patty didn't like him.

"wood ur mom let patty live w u again?" Asa asked.

"4 sure."

"yr mom iz great."

"sometimes. this am she waz raving. sed i looked like a slob."

"u? nevernever."

"she hates the shirt i wore 2day."

"no way. i luv that color, so weird. i am so sorry about patty. she deserves someone great 4 a stepdad. she's been thru enuf already."

"this is tru!"

"my gram sez u can try til the moon turns 2 blu cheez and u wld still never figure y people fall 4 the people they fall 4."

I glanced at the clock: 9:20. "g2g now. luv you."

"luv you 2! c ya. bye."

I waited until ten after ten before I called Cynthia again. She sounded groggy. "Did I wake you up? Are you sleeping?"

"I was, Sarabeth. Not now, obviously."

"Sorry."

"That's okay. What's up?"

"Mom's not home yet."

There was a pause. "What time did you say you got home?"

"It was after five, maybe twenty after."

"And you haven't heard anything from Jane since then?"

"No."

"Okay." Another pause. "Okay," she said again. "Let me call some places. This isn't like Jane. You're right; she's not like this. She never came home this late before, did she?"

"No. No, never."

"Okay, let me call the police, see if they know anything—"

"I can call the police, Cynthia, I can do that." I should have thought of it. Nine one one. Even little four-year-olds knew to do that.

"No, let me do it," Cynthia said.

"Why? I can do it." I wanted to do *something*. I'd been sitting around for hours, just waiting.

"Sarabeth, they might listen to me more— you know what I mean, faster, quicker, what-ever—because I'm an adult. I'll call you back, okay?"

"When?"

"As soon as I know anything. And you call me if she comes in."

I went into Mom's room and lay down on her bed. Tobias padded in after me. "Right here," I said, patting my belly. He leaped up and settled himself, turning a few times.

"Mom has not had a car accident," I said to him. I stroked his ears. "No way. It is just not a possibility."

I was two and a half when my father was killed in a freak accident. Mom always said she was sure that one car accident per family was all God allowed. And if it wasn't God's law, she'd add, then it was the law of Chance. Maybe Chance was also a kind of god. Semigod. Semigod Chance, who was probably even stricter than the real God about things like multiple car accidents in one family.

"Okay, Mom, no car accident. So where are you?" I picked up Tobias and held him close to my face. He was always so warm. I listened for sounds from outside, our car pulling up, the car door slamming, and then Mom's footsteps. . . .

Maybe she had met someone in the market who just had to have her house cleaned today. Maybe this woman was throwing a big party and her regular cleaner was sick. Mom was the kind of person who would go along, even with a stranger, to help her out, and not just for the money, though she'd be glad about that.

I went into the kitchen and filled the kettle again. Whatever had happened to delay Mom, when she came in, she'd want a cup of hot tea with a good squeeze of lemon. I set a cup and saucer at her place and sliced a lemon. Then I replaced the plain white cup I'd put out with a green one that had WORLD'S BEST MOM written on it. It was chipped now, but Mom liked it because I had given it to her for Mother's Day when I was eight years old.

My mind veered back to the ugly, scary car-accident idea. No, no. The World's Best Mom would not have a car accident. The World's Best Mom would not allow that to happen. The World's Best Mom would not be careless. Except that other things besides carelessness caused accidents, things like karma and fate.

No way had carelessness killed my father. A wheel had done that. Two wheels from a truck hauling paving stones had popped off, and one had sped across the highway, as if it was aimed, and crushed the roof of my father's pickup truck.

There was nothing he could have done to stop it. Nothing he could have done to change the outcome, to make what happened turn out any differently. The moment that wheel popped, my father was a dead man, my mother was a widow, and I was a daughter who had lost the chance to ever really know him.

I rearranged the lemon slices so they made a little star and moved the sugar bowl. There, now everything was ready for Mom. No, I'd forgotten a napkin. I folded one of the cloth napkins, the ones we hardly ever used, next to the cup and saucer.

I went to the door and looked out again, wondering if Cynthia could still be talking to the police. "Anyway," I said, as if I were arguing with someone, "Mom is not a good driver; she's an *excellent* driver. She has a clean record, not even a parking ticket."

Leo had once said Mom was the best driver he knew. Then he'd added, in his Leoish way, "After me, of course."

Leo! I should have thought of him right away. I punched in his number, but my fingers slipped and I had to start over. "Leo," I said the instant the phone was picked up. "Is Mom there? Let me speak to her."

"Who is this, please?" a woman asked, her voice twanging with a slightly southern accent. "Who do you want? This is Pepper."

I was momentarily speechless. I had forgotten about her. "This is Sarabeth," I said finally. "Sarabeth Silver. I need to speak to Leo."

"Oh, Sarabeth! Hi, sweetie," she said, as if we'd known each other forever, instead of having met only once. "Hold on; I'll get him."

In a moment, Leo's booming voice filled my ear. "Hey, Sarabee. What's up?"

"Is Mom over there?"

"I haven't seen Jane for weeks, honey."

"Oh." I looked down at my legs. Even in my jeans, they looked too skinny. "Well, the thing is, she didn't come home tonight."

"What are you talking about?"

"Just what I said, Leo. I came home at five, and she wasn't here, and she hasn't called. I thought she might be over at your place."

"That's strange; that's not like her."

"I know, Leo."

"Don't worry, Sarabeth, Jane's got her head

screwed on right. She's not going to do anything dumb."

"Cynthia's calling the police right now. I better hang up, Leo, in case she's trying to get me."

"The police?"

"Yeah, because . . . what if there was an accident?"

"Call me back when she gets home, okay? Or the minute you hear anything. Call me even if it's really late. And don't worry," he said again. "I'm positive there's a perfectly good explanation for this."

I curled up on the red velvet love seat. Mom had bought it at a garage sale last spring. Tobias came padding slowly over and climbed into my lap. "Yes," I said, stroking him, "yes, you nice old boy, you're sick, poor guy." And, sitting there, watching the clock, I tried to think of a perfectly good explanation for Mom's staying out so many hours without calling me.

5

❧

I was sleeping on the couch, my face mashed into a pillow, when the phone ringing woke me. For a moment, I couldn't process where I was, why my face was stuck in a cushion. I wiped my mouth and sat up, overturning Tobias, who had been sleeping on my butt.

The phone was still ringing.

I stumbled into the kitchen. "Hello?"

"I have some information for you," Cynthia said, without any preliminaries.

"What happened? Where's Mom?" I was fully awake now.

"I want you to stay calm. I'm in Trowbridge Hospital. You know the one, up on Seneca Hill—"

"Mom's in the hospital? Then she did have an accident!"

"Don't get upset. I know it sounds bad, and it's not exactly good, but we can—"

"Where did it happen? Was it I-Eighty-one?" My throat constricted. "Did someone smash into her?" The smudgy black-and-white newspaper photo of my father's fatal accident sprang into my mind, only now it wasn't his pickup truck I saw crumpled under that huge wheel, but Mom's rusting two-door Civic.

"It wasn't a car accident, Sarabeth."

"What?"

"She had a heart attack. They found her in the park."

Cynthia had just said something that made no sense. Mom had had a heart attack? People don't have heart attacks when they're twenty-nine years old. They joke about heart attacks, but they don't *have* them. Heart attacks were for old people, frail people, sick people, tense, rich, type A people. Or was it type B? Whatever, it wasn't Mom.

"Sarabeth, are you there?" Cynthia said.

"Yes. . . . "

"She was lying on the ground. They don't know how long she was there in the snow. A man taking a walk found her on one of the paths in the park. You know the place, Millers Park."

"Millers Falls Park," I corrected stupidly. And I remembered how uneasy I'd been all day, how disturbed, as if I knew something was terribly wrong, something I didn't even know I knew.

"Right. Millers Falls Park. That's the one," Cynthia said. "The one near the post office over on Oak Boulevard. They think she was lying there for maybe half an hour before this man found her, and then before the ambulance came, it was even more time. . . ." Her voice trailed away.

"You're in the hospital now?" I said. I kept talking, trying to push away the mental picture of Mom lying on the ground, her face crushed into the snow. I said anything that came to my mind. "Who's staying with Darren? Is it your neighbor, whatsherface? Billy's probably at the base, isn't he?"

"Right, Billy's at the base." Cynthia's voice was low.

"And you're where?" I said again. And it was true that I couldn't remember, although she'd told me only moments ago.

"At Trowbridge Hospital. I've been here for, uh, two hours. It took time for the police to figure out that the woman they'd found was the same person I was asking about. She must have left the car in the parking lot at the park, which they didn't know, of course, so they couldn't trace her that way, and she didn't have any ID on her—"

"Her wallet," I said.

"Right, so they had no idea who this woman was." *This woman . . . the woman they found.* Why was she talking about Mom like that?

I held the phone close to my ear. "What are they doing to her, Cynthia?"

"They're taking care of her, hon. They're giving her the best care, Sarabeth. They've got her in intensive care; people are on the job. It's round-the-clock care. You don't have to worry about that."

"I want to see her," I said. "Why didn't you come and get me before you went to the hospital?"

"I don't know. I guess I should have, but I didn't." Cynthia droned on, her voice without bounce. "I just came straight here; the moment they called I got in the car and drove here, I didn't think of anything else."

"You should have come for me," I said. "You should have come here first."

"Okay, you're right. I'm sorry."

"Come and get me now."

"Now? I can't do that, Sarabeth, I'd be shuttling around all night. Besides, your mom doesn't need company, not now, not in the middle of the night."

"I'm not company, Cynthia." I wrapped the phone cord around my wrist. "I should be there. I should be with her."

"What for? What will you accomplish, except to wear yourself out? Anyway, you can't be with her. They won't let you in." She paused. "I really need to go home now. I've got to get some sleep, and you should, too. Go back to sleep, and in the morning, get up and go to school. Don't stay out of school because of this. You know how Jane is about your missing school. I'll come by and pick you up right after, and we'll zoom over to the hospital. By that time, she should be stabilized."

"I don't want to wait for tomorrow afternoon," I said. "I'll call Suburban Safari. They're on seven/twenty-four. Mom always uses them when the car breaks down."

Last year, when one of the radio stations ran a contest for the "baddest original song lyrics," Mom and I had spent a weekend writing a song together about Suburban Safari. "Suburban Safari went to town, a'riding on its tires. Got three fares and dumped them down," were our opening lines.

We were hoping, wishing, even believing we'd win. The prize was twenty-five dollars, and we could have used it. But somebody else wrote worse lyrics, even though we didn't think it was possible.

"Sarabeth, I'm going to say it once more. Are you listening? Don't come to the hospital now. Jane's completely out of it. All they'd let me do was peek in at her. It would be useless for you to come here. Go back to sleep. That's what your mom would say. You know it! In the morning, we'll talk again. Are you going to be okay?"

"There's nothing wrong with me," I said.

"Right. Okay. You know what time it is?"

I stared at my watch. The numbers glowed up at me. Did they say quarter of one or five after nine? Better, so much better, if it were five after nine. At five after nine, Mom could still walk into the house at any moment. Could still sit down and drink a cup of hot tea with lemon and tell me about her day. At five after nine, I could still be annoyed with her, still be planning how I would remind her that she was the one who was always telling me to let her know where I was and when I'd be home.

When I hung up, I called Trowbridge Hospital. It seemed to take forever to find an actual human who would talk to me, but finally I heard, "Intensive Care Unit. Ed Bowers speaking."

"I'm calling about my mother," I said. "Jane Silver. This is her daughter. Could I speak to a nurse, please?"

"Okay, that's me," Ed Bowers said. "What can I do for you?"

"I want to know how she is."

"She's being watched carefully. She's on the critical list. This is her daughter, you said?"

"Yes. Sarabeth Silver."

"Your mother's in good hands. Dr. Maguire is with her right now. Why don't you call in the morning? I'm sure you can speak to Dr. Maguire or someone else then."

"Yes, I'll do that," I said. I put the phone on the hook and went into Mom's room. I was going to lie down on her bed, but instead, I just stood there looking around and seeing how neat everything was and thinking that doctors had all kinds of drugs and medicine for people these days. People had heart attacks and then they recovered and came home and walked around and did everything they'd always done. They were as good as new. It was so, wasn't it?

I opened her drawers, one after the other, and saw how carefully she had folded everything, neat little stacks of underpants and bras, of shirts and sweaters. She hated the way I threw everything in my drawers helter-skelter; she called them rats' nests. She was always trying to get me to be neater. I made her bed, tucked in the sheets and blankets, punched up the pillow, and pulled the spread smooth.

In the kitchen, I filled the sink with hot water, poured in detergent, and washed the breakfast dishes. I scrubbed each one, holding it under the hot water until it shone. After I finished with the dishes, I scrubbed the sink and wiped down the counters. Then I got the mop and bucket we kept outside in back, filled the bucket with hot water and the all-purpose cleaner Mom used, and mopped the floor. When Mom came home, she'd be impressed. She'd say, "Wow, good job! Thanks!"

We'd hug and kiss, and maybe I'd sit on her lap, which she kept wanting me to do and I kept not wanting to do anymore. But maybe she wouldn't be strong enough to hold me, and I'd tell her to sit on my lap, and she'd laugh, and then she'd do it. Just plunk herself down in my lap, and I'd put my arms around her and hold her as if I was the mom now.

I took the curtains off the window over the sink and put them to soak in the bathtub. Since I was in the bathroom, I mopped that floor, too, and, while I was at it, I cleaned the toilet. My least-favorite job. After that, I rinsed the curtains and hung them over the shower rod to dry.

Tobias padded in, leaving paw prints on the damp floor, and curled up near the hot-water pipe. I sank down next to him, put my hand on his back, and looked into his eyes. Did cats have heart attacks? He blinked and, as his eyes closed, mine did, too. I slept like that, slumped against the wall, for an hour or so; then I woke up, stumbled into my room, and fell across the bed.

6

It was still dark when the coyotes began howling. The air was gray with sleet, and their piercing voices rose and tangled in the air. The coyotes had crossed the border from Canada down into our territory only within the last few years. Mom liked hearing their howls and the kind of scary, thrilled feeling she said it gave her, the reminder that the whole world wasn't civilized. But every night when Tobias went out for his prowl, I worried about his being caught and eaten.

And now the same thought came to me again, only it was of a pack of coyotes coming across Mom lying helpless in the snow.

"No," I said out loud. "No!" I bolted out of bed and walked through the house. That hadn't happened. Mom wasn't lying in the snow anymore. She was safe in the hospital. She was being taken care of.

It was dark outside, still hours before I had to go down to the school bus stop at the foot of the hill, but I showered, washed my hair, got dressed, made my lunch, did everything as if I was getting ready to go to school. I meant to go to school, but what I actually did was call Suburban Safari and ask them to send a taxi to the house.

"How much is it going to be?" I asked the driver, looking into the window.

"You're going up to Trowbridge?" He put his hands flat on the steering wheel. "Didn't they tell you? They shoulda told you when you called." He was an older man with a blank face, as if he had no emotions. "Fifteen," he said.

"Fifteen dollars?" I repeated faintly. I knew I should have asked how much it would be when I called the service. Mom always told me, "Ask first, decide second." I had to tip him, too, which would be another couple of dollars. What I had in my backpack was twelve dollars and fifty-three cents.

"Can you wait a minute more, please?" I said.

"How long you gonna be?"

"Fast." I ran back into the house and took Mom's wallet from the shoulder bag. She had four singles and seventy-three cents in change. I checked her secret pocket—sometimes she'd have a ten-dollar bill in there—but it was empty. She never kept much cash on hand. She said it was worth the three dollars she paid on her basic checking account every month not to be tempted to buy stuff we didn't really need.

I was in the cab and on the way to the hospital before I even thought about how I was going to get back home. "Excuse me." I tapped on the driver's shoulder. "Do you think you could . . ." I hesitated, then plunged in. "Would you be able to wait and take me back home?"

"Why not?" he said. "It'll be the same fare."

"Fifteen dollars?" My heart thundered in my chest. "But I don't have any more money."

"You want me to drive you someplace and you don't have any money? You think I do this for fun?" He never lost the flat look on his face, just sounded annoyed.

"No . . . I'm sorry. Okay. I'll figure some-thing—"

"This is a job. Work. Four-letter word you kids today don't know nothing about."

I found a bus token in the bottom of my backpack. I could probably get downtown with that, then get a transfer. I might have to walk the last few miles from the nearest town to where we lived. Or maybe I'd hitch a ride. I'd done that once, and Mom had been so mad at me, I'd promised never to do it again, but this was an emergency.

Just as he turned up Seneca Hill, the driver looked around at me and said, "So what's the story?"

"I have the money for this trip," I said quickly.

"Hey! Did I say you didn't? Alls I'm asking is what you're going up to the hospital for. You know the Vets Hospital is up there, too, right back of Trowbridge?"

"No, I didn't know that."

"I'm telling you, it's there. It's the place to go if you've been in service to your country. They take care of you. That's where I pester the docs when I have trouble with my leg, this one here."

"What's wrong with your leg?"

"They don't know. All the brains up there, and they got plenty, let me tell you, but they can't tell Chester Jay nothing he don't know already. It hurts; it's painful. Sometimes it's a good day, and sometimes it's not so good. Nerve damage or something, they say. Souvenir from Vietnam.

So who you going to see?"

"My mom."

"What's she sick with?"

"Not sick, exactly. She had a heart attack. . . . Heart attack," I repeated, and I kept wanting to say it. *Heart attack . . . heart attack . . . she had a heart attack.*

"What are you, the baby of the family?" the driver asked.

"No, I'm the only one." I knew what he was thinking, that Mom must be old. "My mom's twenty-nine," I said.

The driver whistled. "She's practically a kid herself. And she got a heart attack? Big smoker, I bet."

"No, she never smoked. She's really healthy and strong. She has a healthy life." Before I knew it, I was telling him everything, about Mom's not being home last night and about Cynthia's call in the middle of the night—the whole story. I didn't mean to do that. It wasn't a bid for sympathy; it just came pouring out.

Chester Jay sort of grunted and drove the rest of the way in silence. I looked out the window and tried not to feel too stupid about what Mom would call "overwagging" my tongue.

Chester Jay drove past a big green sign that said TROWBRIDGE HOSPITAL, then through a row of flaming maples spattered with snow. I got the money ready for him, and as soon as he pulled up in front of the door, I handed it over the seat.

"Okay," he said after counting the bills. "You need a receipt?"

"No, thanks." I swung open the door.

"How long you going to be?"

"I don't know," I said.

"Gimme a ballpark figure."

"Ten minutes, or maybe fifteen." I hitched up my backpack. "Mom's in Intensive Care; they won't let me stay long."

"Come out in twenty minutes and I'll still be here," he said. "I'll drive you back home."

I looked in the window at him. "You will?" I wanted to reach in and hug him, but I was afraid I was going to cry. "Thank you," I managed to say. "Thank you a lot. Really—"

"Okay, okay, okay," he said. "Don't get soppy. Don't thank me. Just get going! Twenty minutes, I said. Hoof it!"

"I'm running," I said, and I did. I ran to the

front door and walked fast to the information desk. I was directed to the fourth floor, Wing B. The walls were painted a creamy yellow, with apple green arrows pointing to the different wings. Wing B, Intensive Care, was behind a closed set of double doors that said KEEP OUT. AUTHOR-IZED VISITORS ONLY.

Six rooms rayed out from a central station, like spokes on a wheel. A number of people were around and behind the station, talking, writing on clipboards, and answering phones. It was so strange, and so familiar, in a way. It was like being caught in the middle of a TV show.

I went up to the station and waited until someone looked up and saw me. Then I asked for Ed Bowers. "Ed's off duty," a nurse said, adjusting her gold-framed glasses. "Can I help you?"

"I came to see my mom, Jane Silver."

"You don't need Ed for that." She went behind the desk and picked up some papers. "Your mother can't have visitors now," she said crisply. "Doctor's orders. But if you just want to look in on her—do you want to do that?"

"Yes, please."

She pointed to one of the rooms, and I went

over and stood in the doorway. That was Mom in the bed, a little lump under the covers, with wires and tubes going in and out of her, and monitors banked up behind her and next to her. I watched the covers, watched the rise and fall of her breathing.

"Mom, it's me, Sarabeth," I said in a near whisper. I wasn't sure if I was allowed to talk to her. "Can you hear me?" She stirred—I was sure of it—made a little movement, like a signal.

"Do you think she knew I was there?" I asked the nurse.

She nodded. "Oh, very likely. Hearing is the last thing to go. Even when they're in a coma, they hear things, and your mom's not in a coma. Just a deep sleep. You can think of it that way. She's just having herself a good restful sleep."

All the way home, sitting in the stuffy backseat of Chester Jay's taxi, I thought about how much Mom needed that good restful sleep. Maybe this was the vacation she was always wishing for and never getting.

Just as Chester Jay made the turn onto Stonecutter Road, I heard Mom saying, "I'm okay, babykins. Listen to me. I'm okay." It had been years since she had called me babykins, but I knew it was her voice I'd heard. And I remembered a long time ago—maybe I was four years old—the two of us in the zoo, running down a flight of shallow wooden steps, Mom losing her footing and falling, me flinging myself onto her sprawled body, screaming. And Mom saying, "I'm okay, babykins. Listen to me. I'm okay!"

I remembered, too, how I had taken those words into my mind and held them there, like precious things, and how I had put my arm around Mom's waist, and how she had laughed as she limped toward the car and called herself a klutz and me a big silly for worrying so much.

And then, when Chester Jay stopped in front of our house, I remembered something else, not from long ago, but from yesterday morning. How Mom had almost had to beg me for a kiss. How I had bent over and stingily, for an instant only, let my lips touch her cheek.

7

"I wonder if Patty's sick," Asa said, meeting me in the hall between classes. "She's absent today. Maybe she got the flu, too, like Grant."

"Maybe," I said, straightening up from the water fountain.

"You're looking sort of pale yourself." Asa fiddled with her braids. "Are you okay?"

"I don't know." I stared down at my sneakers. Why had I put on black high-tops? I couldn't remember doing it. "My mom's in the hospital," I said. "I went to see her this morning."

"No way! Has she got the flu, too? My mom said it can be serious for some people."

"Heart attack."

"What? What'd you say?"

I nodded. My eyes filled.

"Your mom had a heart attack?" Asa said. "She's way young for that, Sarabeth. Are you sure? Did a doctor say that?"

The bell rang then. I walked away without saying anything else. I couldn't. Asa called after me, but I just went on up the stairs.

Later that morning, in the middle of social studies class, a call came over the intercom. "Sarabeth Silver." It was Mrs. Coppel. "Come to the office right away. Your mother . . . Sarabeth Silver, come to the office."

"Okay, go on," Mr. Abdo said. "If your mother's here, I suppose it's more important than this."

Mom was here? I went fast down the hall. I ran toward the stairs. I almost jumped into the air and clicked my heels together. Only a few hours ago, Mom had been lying in a hospital bed in the ICU, but she was strong—strong and stubborn. I could see her waking up, deciding she'd spent enough time in the hospital, pulling out all the tubes and junk they'd stuck in her, and pulling on her clothes. She'd be thinking she had things to do, people counting on her. Taking the stairs two at a time, I saw it all—Mom moving through the hospital lobby, out the door, taking in a big gulp of cold air, deciding that the first thing she had to do was to see me.

I really knew it couldn't be so, but I wanted to believe it.

In the office, Mrs. Coppel was at her desk behind the high counter. "Sarabeth," she said, her voice deepening, and she half stood up. I looked around. There were two other women working behind the counter, and both had stopped work on their computers and were watching me. The only other person there was a girl slumped on the bench near Mr. Dunsenay's door.

No Mom.

Mrs. Coppel pushed her oversized red-frame glasses up on her head. "Sarabeth," she said again. She came to the counter, carrying the phone with its long spiraled cord. "You have a phone call, dear."

"Is it my mother?"

"I . . . don't think so." She patted my arm. Her hand was warm, almost hot.

I took the phone from her. "Hello." Then, still thinking it could be Mom, I said, "Mom, is that you? Where are——"

"It's me," Cynthia interrupted. "I'm coming over to get you now, Sarabeth. I should be there in fifteen minutes. Wait outside for me."

"Cynthia, are you with Mom?"

"It's okay for you to leave school now," she

said. "I talked to someone in the office there, your principal, I think. Go outside and wait for me," she said, and hung up.

I hardly had to explain anything to Mrs. Coppel. I just started to say my mother was in the hospital. "Yes, I know," she said, and she wrote out a pass for me to give to Mr. Abdo. "Good luck, dear," she said, and gave my arm another warm pat.

Almost the moment I walked out the front door, Cynthia pulled up to the curb in her VW Bug, the same rusting black winter rat she'd had forever. The windshield wipers were clearing out the sleety stuff that was still falling.

Cynthia leaned over and cranked the handle on the passenger side. You couldn't open that door from the outside anymore.

"We're going straight to the hospital?" I asked, sliding in. Not really a question.

"Yeah," Cynthia said. Then she said, in a determined way, "No, actually. No, we're not."

I looked at her, unsure if she was serious or playing with me. She had been a bar singer and acted in local theater a few times, and she could be a drama queen.

"I went to the hospital by taxi this morning,"

I said. "A Suburban Safari guy took me. He was really nice. Cynthia, I didn't have the money for going back home, but—"

"So you did it," she interrupted.

I nodded. "You were right, though. All they'd let me do was stand in the doorway and look at Mom. She was flat out asleep. Is she awake now? You wouldn't believe . . . I got stupid and thought she was actually discharged and coming to school for me." I gave a weird-sounding laugh, more like a cough.

Cynthia just sat there, gripping the steering wheel with both hands. She looked different somehow, half-asleep, or as if something had scared her, only she was never scared of anything. Maybe it was her messy hair that made her look strange, or maybe it was the yellow slicker she was wearing, probably Billy's, and way too big for her.

"We have to talk," she said after a moment. "We have to talk about some, some uh, some stuff."

I dropped my backpack on the floor, corralled it between my feet. "Let's go. We can talk as we drive."

She pulled into traffic, but then just moseyed

along like an old-man driver. "Can you drive faster, please," I said.

"Sure," she said, but she didn't. "We should talk," she said again.

"Talk about what?" My throat was dry. "Oh, I know," I sang out, being half cute, half serious. "Money! Money! I know! Okay, so we don't have health insurance! So we can't pay the bill straight off! *So what*? What's the hospital going to do, make Mom wash dishes before they let her out?" My heart skittered around in my chest. I hadn't actually thought until that moment about the hospital bill. How would we ever pay it off?

"What, you guys don't have health insurance?" Cynthia said.

"I thought you knew that, Cynthia! You know all our secrets. No money, no Leo, no health insurance."

"You okay, Sarabeth?" Cynthia turned to look at me. "Don't melt down on me."

"I'm fine." I found a hard candy in my pocket and stuck it in my mouth. "You know what Mom always says—'We can't afford to get sick, so we just won't.'" As soon as I said it, I wished I hadn't. That was as absurd as trying to convince myself that Mom had been waiting for me in the office.

"'So we just won't,'" Cynthia echoed in a little voice that was completely unlike her. She slid through a light turning red and made a bumpy left turn onto Linkline Road. Big houses, huge lawns. She was crying.

"Cynthia?" I said.

She pulled over to the side of the road, next to a pair of stone lions on pedestals. "Sarabeth, I don't know how to say this. . . . Jane is . . ." She turned the ignition key off, then on again. "I can't talk in the car," she said.

"I don't want to talk now, anyway. Let's go! I want to see Mom." I reached over, put my foot on the gas pedal, floored it, and the car, still in gear, leaped forward.

"Hell!" Cynthia shouted, and kicked my foot off the pedal. She pulled the keys out of the ignition and threw them on the dashboard. "They couldn't resuscitate her," she said, and she covered her face with both hands.

I knew what *resuscitate* meant, but I couldn't get it clearly into my mind. It was something about breathing. Breathing into another person's mouth? For instance, if you were swimming and swallowed water, and then you were gagging and choking—no, no, gagging and choking was when they pounded you on the back. Or was it the chest? Or was that when you swallowed something and it got stuck in your throat? No again—that was when they grabbed you around the middle and squeezed. The Heimlich maneuver.

There was something else, another procedure, if your heart stopped. *That* was when they pounded you on the chest. They would pound you with fists, maybe break your ribs doing it, but that didn't matter, because if they didn't pound you, you would die.

All at once, the lights went on everywhere in the enormous house at the top of the enormous lawn we were parked in front of. The chattering voice in my mind commented that lights made any house, even a big one, look cozy. Maybe I should walk up the long, long driveway, knock on the big, big door, and tell the woman who answered that my mom was in the hospital, and ask if I could use her phone to call there? The woman would be sympathetic, concerned. She'd tell me to sit down. She'd bring me a glass of water with a lemon slipped over the edge. She'd punch in the number for me, get right through to Mom, and hand me the phone. She'd probably have white leather couches and big vases of fresh flowers everywhere.

Flowers! I should have bought flowers for Mom. That's what you did when someone was in the hospital. You took flowers to the hospital, and then got more to welcome her when she came home. Flowers were expensive, but it didn't matter. Maybe I'd even buy roses, yellow roses, which Mom loved.

A long time seemed to have passed since Cynthia had said the *r* word. But how long could it have been? Here we were, still sitting in the car, and there was Cynthia, still covering her face and making those sounds, and here I was, still thinking these useless thoughts. Cynthia raised her head. Blue eyeliner was smeared down one cheek.

"Sarabeth . . ." Her voice squeaked into a sob. She reached out her arms to me. "Why do I have to tell you this? She had another heart attack this morning. Oh, Sarabeth. Oh, poor baby. Oh . . . Jane . . . she, she . . . she's dead. She died." Her lips trembled.

"You're crazy," I said. I fumbled for the door

handle. "You're really crazy, and I'm not staying here with you."

I got out of the car and began walking. I'd go to the hospital myself.

I'd tell Mom about Cynthia's blurting out that she had died. Mom would get a laugh out of that, remind me that Cynthia had a tendency to jump the gun. "You think I'd drop out on you like that?" she'd say. "Can't get rid of me that easy!"

I should have gone up to the stone-lion house. The nice woman would have driven me to the hospital in her Mercedes-Benz. She had to have a Mercedes. All rich people had a Mercedes, or maybe even two. One would be a little sports car that was just for her. We'd get in and she'd zip past all the traffic. Get me to the hospital in record time. She would probably go right up to Mom's room with me.

The VW horn bleated behind me, seemed to bleat out the word *resuscitate*. Strange word. It lodged itself in my mind. That whispery *sus* sound and then *citate*, so crackly and crisp. I walked faster. Cars passed, tires crackling over the road, the sound of cornflakes. Cornflakes! I had to tell Mom that one; she'd get a laugh out of that, too.

The VW moved slowly, half on the road, half on the shoulder. A horn blasted, and one of those big vans swung out into the passing lane, past Cynthia's little car. The Bug pulled up next to me. Cynthia reached over and swung open the passenger door. "Sarabeth," she called.

I got in the car. Cynthia reached for my hand. "It was quick. She didn't suffer, sweetie."

Sweetie. What Mom called me sometimes. "Don't talk to me," I said. "Please, just go."

I slumped back against the seat, my eyes closed, listening to the sound of the tires vibrating on the road.

8

"Do you have your keys?" Cynthia asked, pulling up in front of our house. I got out without answering.

Inside, Tobias met us, pushing out his back legs. I knelt and looked in his face. I'd read that cats could warn people of earthquakes, that they became terribly agitated and insisted that attention be paid. But then, why not heart attacks? "Couldn't you have warned us?" I whispered hotly at him. My neck ached, and I wanted to shake him. He blinked, then turned away from me, as if he could smell my anger.

"You need something hot to drink," Cynthia said. She took off the yellow slicker, hung it over the back of a chair. "I'll make you a cup of tea; then you can get some things together." She filled the kettle and put it on the stove. "You don't have to take everything now, just enough for a few days."

I sat down and fiddled with a spoon, tapping it slowly on the table. *Tap . . . tap . . . tap. . . .* The

68

table was still set for Mom from last night. "I told you, Cynthia, I'm not going with you." All the way home, we'd argued about where I was going to sleep tonight. Cynthia wanted me to go to her house. I wanted to stay right here. "You're not going to pry me out of here," I said.

"Sarabeth, you can't stay here alone, not tonight, of all nights. You've been through too much to be alone." She picked up the World's Best Mom cup and turned it between her hands. "She was, wasn't she?" she said, and she started talking about the time we all went camping at Roger's Rock in the Adirondacks.

I knew she wanted to distract me. She thought I was out of my mind right now—yelling at her in the car that I *would* stay in my own house—and maybe I was crazed, but I still wasn't going with her.

"I'm staying here," I said for about the tenth time. "Here. Right here. My house."

"I want tea, too," she said, as if I hadn't spoken, and opened the cupboard. "Tomato soup. Corn-flakes. Tuna fish. Where's the tea? Just herbal tea? Did Jane like that stuff?"

"It was for Leo." The rye sesame crackers she

was taking out had been for Leo, too. They were probably stale by now. "The regular tea's on the bottom shelf."

"Oh, right." She came back to the table and dropped a tea bag in each cup. "We have to call Leo, let him know. Who else? We should draw up a list."

A list of who we should politely call and let know about Mom? Bizarre. Everything was bizarre. Sitting here was bizarre. Making tea when Mom was dead was bizarre. I grabbed the tea-kettle, tipped the spout over the cups. Boiling water splashed out.

"Watch it," Cynthia cried.

I threw down a handful of napkins to soak up the spilled water, then sat down and dumped spoonfuls of sugar into my cup. The tea tasted awful.

Cynthia sat down next to me. "I just can't believe it," she said, and then she was crying.

I chewed on my thumbnail, biting and ripping. I didn't want to look at Cynthia, at her scrunched-up face, wet and slimy with tears. And I didn't want to hear her, the way she was crying in rhythmic bursts, almost like singing. "Ahhh . . .

ahhh . . . ahhhh . . ." I couldn't stand it. I didn't even want her to be here. I hit the saltshaker with the back of my hand, knocked it over. Dead saltshaker. I hit the pepper shaker, knocked it to the floor. Dead pepper shaker. I swept the sugar bowl off, and it shattered into pieces. Dead sugar bowl.

Cynthia stared at me. "Take it easy," she said. She wiped her face with a napkin. "I'll clean that up, don't worry."

Fine. I wasn't worrying. What was there to worry about anymore? I poured my tea into the sink. Good that Mom wasn't here to see me wasting food. A weak sun broke through the clouds. Mom always said it was a great thing to have a window over the sink, where you spent so much time.

"Where's Mom's car?" I asked.

"I'm not sure." Cynthia tipped the sugar bowl fragments into the garbage can. "Cops probably have it. I'll check on it. Go get some clothes together. Don't forget your toothbrush. Oh, who can we get to watch Tobias? One of your neighbors, or how about Leo?"

I thought of Mom in her room, crying over

Leo. I took the box of rye crackers and threw it in the garbage can. If Leo were here, I'd throw the box at him. I'd hit him with all the boxes and cans in the cupboard, and then I'd beat him with my fists, make him cry the way Mom had cried.

"I told you enough times, Cynthia. I'm not going with you, and if I were, I wouldn't ask Leo to watch Tobias."

Cynthia took her cup to the sink and rinsed it. "Sarabeth," she said, putting the cup in the drain. "Listen to me once more. You cannot stay here alone."

"I've stayed alone before, plenty of times." I was proud how calm I sounded. Yesterday morning when Mom had been upset, I'd been calm, too, sitting with my feet hooked over the chair rung, mushing up my cornflakes, while Mom ranted on about vio-*lent* colors of*fend*ing her eyes. I smiled. Mom could be funny.

"You're not thinking straight, honey." Cynthia gripped my arm. "This is not an ordinary time. You should not be alone now. Go and get your things, and don't be stubborn."

Her soft, whispery voice had deserted her, and my so-called calm deserted me. "Be quiet,

Cynthia! I don't want you to speak to me. I don't want to hear your voice. I don't want to hear anything else!" I wrenched away from her.

In the living room, I sat on the little red velvet couch, wrapped in the afghan Mom had bought last spring, at the same garage sale where we bought the couch. The couch had been sitting outside on a newly tarred driveway with a bunch of chairs. Mom had gotten down on her hands and knees to check out the springs, her blue-jeaned butt sticking up in the air, as if she could care less what anybody thought.

"Look, we've got to stop fighting about this." Cynthia sat down next to me. She was too close, her breath too warm. "It's horrible now, but it will be okay. I'm telling you, it will be okay in time."

For a moment, her voice soothed me. I sagged against her. I wanted to believe her. I was so tired.

But then she went into my room and started taking clothes out of the drawers—underwear, socks, shirts. "You don't need much," she said, "just a few things." As fast as she took stuff out, I put it back.

73

All at once, she sat down on my bed. "Sarabeth, we've been doing this for two hours! Okay, okay, you win. I'm not going to drag you out of here by your hair. And I need to go home, I've left Darren with my neighbor too long."

She went into the kitchen and put on her slicker. "Your mom always said you were stubborn. I just didn't know how stubborn. I'll call you in the morning," she said, and she left.

I lay down on the couch again and fell asleep instantly. When I woke, it was dark and silent, and I was struggling out of the folds of the afghan, my heart snapping in my chest as if it was a zipper and someone was yanking it up and down, up and down.

"Mom," I cried out, and then I was listening for the rattle of her car, for her footsteps coming fast up the walk, for the kitchen door creaking open and the thud of her boots as she kicked them off.

Listening for her to call out, "Where are you? Anything good happen in school today? I want to hear about it!"

I rolled off the couch onto the floor and buried my face in my arms. "Sarabeth, what are you doing? Get up off that floor."

I could hear Mom saying it.

I'm thinking, Mom, I told her in my mind. I'm thinking about that wheel that killed my father. Do you believe it was marked for him, written in the stars? And your heart attack, how about that? Actually, I know you don't believe in that stuff. Neither do I, but then I don't believe you're dead, either. You're not the dead kind, Mom; you're the alive kind. Did you know that there were people who used to believe that when someone died, the soul jetted right up to the stars, settled down, and watched over the ones left behind? I hope your soul is watching over me, Mom. Are you on the job? Could you answer me, please?

Toward morning, the wind came up, rattling the windows. Something clanked against the wall outside. I had been sleeping on the floor with Tobias tight against my ribs. He lifted his head, his ears stiff. "If you're listening for her, forget it," I said. "She's not coming home. We're alone now. Don't you know that?" I picked him up, grabbed him around his belly. I was too rough, and he squealed like a pig.

"I'm sorry," I said. I kissed his face, and he wriggled to get out of my grip. "Okay," I said, releasing him. "Don't worry, though, you're not going to be alone. Not you. It's me. I'm alone." A door opened in my mind and that word entered. *Alone*. It marched in, sat down, and the door slammed shut.

I'd been alone before, but this was different. Before, I'd always known that Mom was coming, that in two or three or four hours, she'd be home. Before, *alone* had been like a little path with the end in plain sight. This *alone* was like being in a box. A sealed-in place. No opening. No air. No way out. This was *alone* without an ending.

9

"Chips, dip, sodas, coolers, beer," Billy enumerated, emptying grocery bags onto the kitchen table. He took off his cap and slapped it against his leg. He was wearing his army uniform. His face was wet, his hair plastered to his forehead.

"Pouring wet snow out there again," he said. "What do you say, girls, should I have bought another six-pack of diet Coke?"

"Looks good to me," Cynthia said.

We were holding an open house for the neighbors. Cynthia's idea. "They all knew your mom," she said. "We have to do it."

I said okay, fine. When she said we should phone the people Mom had cleaned for and tell them, I said okay, fine. I said okay, fine to everything. Even when she told me after the first night that I had to go sleep at her place. Okay, fine.

All afternoon, people came in, stamping snow off their boots and handing Cynthia and me bowls of food and sometimes flowers. Some people looked around, as if they expected to see Mom, and then they'd see me, and their faces would go all loose and teary. They put out their arms and held me and patted me. The things they said blended together in my mind, as if they were one long, pitying wail. "... poor thing ... poor girl ... now you have to be strong ... have to be brave ..."

Later, I couldn't remember anything I'd said, or if I'd said anything at all. I did remember, once, looking at my feet, surprised at their large size. And I remembered not knowing where to put my hands. Should they be clasped demurely in front of me? Or maybe behind me, the prisoner pose, or should they be crossed over my chest?

My dress had long sleeves and a straight skirt. Mom and I both hated it, but it was the darkest thing I had, and Cynthia said I had to wear something dark. It was a rule. I wished I knew the other rules on how to behave when your mother died. Someone should really write a book on what to wear, what to do with your hands, and if smiles were okay or forbidden. What about tears? Okay to skip until you were alone?

The door opened and closed continuously.

Waves of cold air rushed in. Billy offered food and opened soda bottles. Coats, hats, and scarves piled up on the bed and the chair in my room. Suddenly, though, I noticed that people were using Mom's bed, too. I gathered armfuls of coats and scarves and threw them into my room. I closed Mom's door. It was warped and had never shut easily. I pulled it hard into place.

Someone took me by the arm, turned me around. "Sarabeth, your poor mommy." It was Mrs. Chung, one of the neighbors Mom was sort of friendly with. "Are you going to be okay?" Mrs. Chung said, holding me at arm's length and staring into my face. "What will you do now, poor thing?"

Howl. Scream. Knock my fist through the window. Bash my head against the wall. Stand guard in front of Mom's door forever.

Mrs. Chung shook her finger at me. "You can't be a little girl anymore. Got to grow up."

I nodded, thinking that if she knew my thoughts, she'd shake her finger twice as hard. I paced through the house. I couldn't sit still. I roamed from the kitchen to the living room, to my room, and back to the kitchen. Every room was jammed with people. Every table and counter was burdened with bowls of food. And every particle of air was filled with words. "*Shocked . . . couldn't believe . . . paper said . . . heart . . . sudden . . . tragic. . . .*"

At one point, I sat down, then instantly stood up, as if the chair, one that Mom had never liked, had ejected me. Then I sat down on the floor, but that was no good, either. Drove Mom nuts when I sprawled on the floor. I sat on the red couch. That was always good. I'm like Goldilocks. An amusing thought. Would it be okay to laugh?

I kept my feet flat on the floor, hands in my lap, and people started bending down to speak to me, almost bowing, as if I was royalty now. Their voices were hushed, their eyes watery, sometimes curious and sometimes, I thought, frightened. I didn't like looking at the scared eyes.

"I heard it on the radio," Dolly Krall boomed at me. She and her husband, Fred, owned the trailer court. She didn't have scared eyes. "WDNY, five o'clock news. Twenty-nine-year-old woman dies of heart attack. And I said to Fred, 'No way! Too young.' Then, don't ask why, but Jane Silver's name jumped smack into my mind. I never thought I had ESP before! So, how is Sarabeth doing?"

How *is* Sarabeth doing? Quite well, actually. Feels as if she's in a cave, looking out. No one's looking in; no one sees her. They only think they do.

"I'm Alison Milleritz," a woman in a puffy green coat said. "I knew your mother. She was wonderful, such a strong woman."

She went away and another woman, wearing slacks and big silver earrings, stood in front of me. "We live over there," she said, pointing. "My kids go to school with you. Ricky Albertson and Shawness Albertson." She said her husband was here, too, and she pointed at him. He was talking to Fred Krall. "Mitch," she called, and he came over and patted my shoulder.

I thanked them both for coming. I was doing better about talking. I answered some questions. I said I was fine. I said not to worry about me. This was the way Mom would want me to speak, in control, good manners, no crying. Never cry in public. One of Mom's "Rules of Life."

Old Mr. Symborska bent over me, thin and shaking. Ever since I was a little girl, whenever he saw me, he'd break into song: "You are my sunshine, my only sunshine . . ." And then ask if I'd marry him when I grew up. But now, he just said my name and sighed deeply, and I wondered if we were thinking the same thing, that he was so old and still going on, but Mom, so young, was gone.

Suddenly, Jennifer and Patty were there, one on each side of me, hugging me, crying, saying my name. "Sarabeth . . . Sarabeth, oh, it's so awful . . . so unfair . . . Sarabeth. . . ."

I couldn't speak. I drew in a deep, shaking breath. "Please stop." My eyes filled. "Please don't cry here. Please don't."

"Mr. Dunsenay made an announcement about your mom," Jennifer said, blinking and looking at me from wet eyes.

"What? The principal? He talked about me?"

Patty nodded and looked down at my hand, taking it and touching each fingernail, one after the other.

"He told us over the intercom," Jennifer said. "He told us about . . . about your mom."

There was something in her voice that reminded me of Mrs. Coppel's when she had handed me the phone in the office. I remembered her saying my name. And then, afterward, in the car, Cynthia saying my name, the same pulsating note in her voice that had been in Mrs. Coppel's, that was in Jennifer's now. I knew what that sound was now—pity. Pity, and something else, too. Fear.

"Poor child." The pitying voice seemed to speak right out of my mind, but it was Patty's mother, whispering, hugging me against her chest. She smelled so good, like roses, and for a moment, all I wanted was to stay there in her embrace, breathing in the delicious smell of her perfume. Real perfume, the stuff that came in a tiny crystal bottle and cost more for a single ounce than Mom earned in a month.

I stood and walked away. I traveled through the house again. Room to room to room. Everywhere, people were clustered, eating and talking, laughing, telling stories. It was a party. Maybe I was the guest of honor, or was it Mom? Could the guest of honor be missing? It was hot in the house, noisy, crowded. I wanted to get out, get away, go someplace cold and fresh and quiet.

I went outside and stood by the kitchen door. Snow was falling, sticking to my hair, melting as it hit the ground. Just as Billy had said, snowy rain. Or did he say rainy snow? Whatever. I was getting wet, and that was good. I wanted to get wet. I wanted to get soaked, the way Mom and I had been soaked on the night she woke me up.

"Sarabeth, there you are! Get back inside here." Dolly Krall clamped her hand on my arm and half dragged me back into the house. "You want to catch your death of cold? You want to follow your mother?" She slammed the door. "Cynthia, here, tells me your mom wanted to donate her organs. Liver, kidney, eyes, everything. Good for her. I congratulate her. Hey. Don't look so pasty about it; it didn't happen."

"Jane wanted it," Cynthia said, putting her arm around my waist. "Her donor card was in her wallet. She always carried it, but it turns out they only take organs from people on life support."

"Oh, the ones that have been in car accidents and whatnot," Dolly Krall said. "That's right, I knew that. My cousin Mariel, her name's like that actress Mariel whachamacallit, only the actress is good-looking and my cousin's homely as a post, but she got a kidney from a donor who smashed up on I-Eighty-one. Whole new life for my cousin."

Later—I wasn't sure how much time had passed—I found myself sitting across from Leo at the kitchen table. He kept looking at me, as if he was trying to find the answer to some big problem in my face. He was sort of a funny-looking guy—big chest; little waist; short, skinny bowed legs; but then there were his eyes, deep brown eyes, with long, girlie lashes.

"Pepper and I have been talking," he said. "We think you should crash with us until we all can dope things out for you."

It was the way we'd sat a hundred—no, a thousand other times. Me and Leo . . . and Mom. Leo talking, me doing homework, Mom painting her sneakers white or mending a blouse. But now it was Pepper sitting here, not Mom. Pepper, wearing a long black skirt, lifting an arm covered with thin silver bracelets.

"You listening, Sarabeth?" Leo said. "We gotta figure out what you're going to do. We don't want you to worry about anything; we're going to hang with you all the way." The same thing Cynthia had said, only in Leospeak. "Just count on staying with us until you get sorted out."

Pepper nudged him. "Leo, that sounds as if Sarabeth's a pack of cards that needs to be reshuffled."

Cute, but if she hadn't been there, I could have said it and laughed with Leo. I tried to think of a funny remark, but the phone rang then, and it was for me. Asa and Grant calling.

They both started crying. "Sorry to be so predictable," Asa sobbed. Grant cried softly, hoarsely, in the background.

My eyes throbbed and burned. I forced myself to think of the miracle of their tears traveling over the long, looping wire across the city from their eyes to my ear. The world was so full of miracles. Telephone miracle. TV miracle. Computer miracle. Only, no miracle for Mom.

10

"Sarabeth might as well just stay on with us," Cynthia said. "She's got to sleep on the couch, but hey! It's comfortable, isn't it?" she said, looking at me. I nodded. "Anyway," she said, "I'm sure that's what Jane would have wanted. I don't mean the couch! I mean living with us. And Billy and I have already talked about it and, well, we're ready."

"We are," Billy confirmed, tipping back in his chair.

"So, good, but Sarabeth could come to us, too," Leo said, looking at Pepper. "We have a pretty big place we're renting, and Jane didn't leave any kind of written instructions, did she?"

Everyone had finally left, but the four of them had remained to clean up and, I realized now, to discuss me. What I should do, where I should go, who I should live with. Nobody had asked me anything yet.

I put a jelly glass in the cupboard, bumped another one next to it, and said, "I'll stay right here."

"Don't be silly, Sarabeth. You can't do that," Cynthia said.

"Not an option," Leo agreed, booming, his voice matching Cynthia's rich voice, as if they were both onstage. But they were standing at the sink. She was washing dishes; he was drying.

"I think it is an option," I said. "I want to stay in my own house."

"You can't stay alone," Leo said. "Not to speak of how are you going to buy food, pay the rent and the other bills."

"She knows that," Cynthia said. "We've already been over this whole thing."

"I can figure it out," I said. "I'll get a part-time job. I can take care of myself. Why do I have to go anyplace else?"

"Ha!" Billy said in his army sergeant's voice, calling us all to attention. "Are you out of your mind, Sarabeth?"

"You're a girl," Leo chimed in, as deep-voiced and loud as Billy, "a fifteen-year-old kid. You're not staying here alone."

I sat down, dizzy, the contrasts between them too sharp for my eyes, too loud for my ears. Cynthia operatically singing her words, Leo like the god of thunder booming his, and Pepper with her thin arms and jingling silver bracelets, and Billy with his *Ha!*'s and his sharply cut hair and perfectly pressed khakis.

"Even if it was a possibility, to let you stay here would be a total desecration of Jane's memory," Cynthia said, turning around from the sink. She peered at me from her height, which suddenly seemed impossibly tall. "Can you imagine what Jane would say about your being alone and not putting school first?"

"She would go nuts," Leo confirmed.

"That's putting it mildly," Cynthia said. "We all know how Jane felt about school. She revered education!" She lit a cigarette. She'd given up smoking when she was pregnant with Darren, but she was at it again. "Do you really think any of us could sleep, Sarabeth, knowing you were here all by yourself? And even if we would consider it, which none of us would, the county would not allow it."

"The who?" I said.

"The county. Your legal parent now, Sarabeth. Sorry to say it this way, sweetie, but you're an orphan."

"Little Orphan . . . Sarie?" I said, making a feeble joke. Only Leo responded, giving me a grin and flipping the dish towel at me.

"You're grieving, Sarabeth," Pepper said suddenly. She'd been quiet until then, wrapping the leftover food in foil. She gave me a solicitous look. "You shouldn't be solitary; it's not a healthy thing."

I didn't want to hear her say anything, but give her this much—she didn't say it twenty-five times over, like the others did. In the end, I shut up and let them all go at it, let them ask the questions and bat around the answers. Their answers.

Should Sarabeth live with Leo and Pepper or with Cynthia and Billy? Hmmm, gotta think about that one. What should they do with Jane's stuff, store it or call the Rescue Mission? Store it for now, too soon to make these decisions. What about money? Jane didn't have any. For her, it was touch and go every month. Would there be a refund of the rent? Pul-leeze, did you get a load of Dolly Krall's face? That woman is tight as a fist. But Sarabeth will get Social Security now, won't she, something like Aid to Dependent

Children? So who's going to oversee it? And what about Jane's car? Oh, we can talk about that later on.

I hated this talk, hated every bit of it. I left the kitchen and went into Mom's room. I lay down on her bed. Her sheets and pillow smelled like her, not like expensive roses, nothing like that, just a good Mom smell. I couldn't describe it, but I knew it, and I pressed my face into her pillow.

"Sarabeth?" I must have drowsed. Cynthia was at the door. "Come on in the kitchen, hon; we need to talk to you."

I sat down between Cynthia and Leo. I felt closest to them, but not really close, either, not the way I used to be. They all looked at me, solemn-faced, as if they expected me to speak, to say something profound. "What?" I said.

Leo and Cynthia started talking at the same time. "We've decided . . . this is the thing . . . you see . . . "

"Hold it!" Billy used his sergeant voice. "One at a time."

Cynthia told me that I was going to live with her and Billy. They didn't have the room for me, as I knew, but they were married, and Leo and Pepper weren't. "They're respectable folk; we aren't," Leo joked. "Not yet, anyway."

"What about Tobias?" I said.

There was silence for a moment; then Cynthia said, "Oh, shoot. We forgot the cat."

"We're not taking him," Billy said.

I half rose. "Tobias has to come with me." My voice cracked with panic.

"Sarabeth, you know our place," Cynthia said. "You know how much room we have. I mean, how much room we don't have."

Pepper picked up Tobias and held him near her chin. "Is he sick, Sarabeth?"

"He's got . . . a cold." I could barely get out the words. Not have Tobias with me? We'd always been together.

"He's sweet." Pepper stroked him, her bracelets rattling. "I love this little orange bit over his eye."

"His fur usually looks much better," I said. "Like clean, clean white snow. And he's really much livelier, even if he is getting old. And he understands people, he really does. He's very——" I broke off. I didn't know why I was talking so much.

"I'd take him to live with us," Pepper said.

"How about it, Leo? Let's take him, okay?"

"Oh. Sure," Leo said. He didn't sound that enthusiastic, but it was settled—Tobias's fate, and mine.

11

Mom died on Friday. That was the day I saw her in the hospital and the night I stayed alone. Saturday was the first night I slept over at Cynthia and Billy's place. Sunday was the open house and the second night I slept over at Cynthia and Billy's place, but the first night I officially moved in with them.

Monday was the beginning of a new week, as Cynthia pointed out. I stayed out of school. I wasn't ready to go back yet. I stayed out on Tuesday, too. That was the day Mom was cremated. Mrs. Corelli called at 8:15, and Cynthia spoke to her. Then around ten o'clock, the phone rang again. "Get that, will you?" Cynthia called. "I'm in the bathroom."

It was Mr. Keller from the funeral home. "Ms. Silver," he said. "How are you? I know you will want to pick up your mother's remains, and you may do it any day now. How would tomorrow be?"

"No," I said.

"Well, then, when would be good for you?"

I was silent.

"Friday?"

"No."

"Do you want to suggest a day?"

Again I was silent. The day I wanted to suggest was no day. Never. I didn't want to pick up Mom's "remains."

"How about a week from Thursday?" Mr. Keller was saying. "Surely you can make it then? And we'll settle the financial arrangements at that time, so of course Mrs. Ramos will be with you."

I called Cynthia to set the time with Mr. Keller. While she was on the phone, I played with Darren and didn't let myself think about anything else. "Horsie," Darren said, and I got down on the floor so he could climb on my back. He was a chunky little guy with big hands. Billy joked that he was going to be a truck driver or a boxer. "He's got the hands for it," he'd say, then irritate Cynthia by adding, "He got them straight from his mom."

Later that afternoon, Cynthia asked if I wanted to go out for a walk with her and Darren. "You should come with us," she said, zipping up

Darren's puffy jacket and buckling his little snow boots. Same thing she'd said the day before.

"No, thanks." Same thing I'd said the day before.

"All you've been doing is sitting around, Sarabeth. Your mom would really not like that."

"Is there something you want me to do?" I asked. "I can vacuum or wash the blinds or—"

"No, I don't mean that sort of thing!"

"I don't mind."

"Just forget it. I want you to do things for yourself. Okay, I'm going to indulge you today: You lie around or whatever you want to do, but tomorrow I expect you to pick yourself up and get in the groove. That means school. And right now, maybe you could do something, after all, like folding the blankets, so the couch doesn't look like a tornado just whirled through here."

"Oh, sure," I said, but after she left, I just sat at the window, staring down into the street. It was so different from where I'd lived with Mom. There, it had been all young families and old people, and I pretty much knew everyone, at least by sight. Cynthia and Billy lived on a busy main street. You could just sit there and not think of anything, just watch the cars and the crowds of people always going up and down the street and in and out of the buildings.

Time passed. I don't know if I was actually thinking or just vegetating, but when the phone rang, the sound went through me like a needle. The ringing didn't stop, and I finally went into the kitchen to answer.

"Silver!" It was Jen. "Where were you? I was just going to hang up."

"Sorry, Jen."

"Everyone's with me. We're all here at my house, and we decided to call you. Patty had Cynthia's number. Good thing, huh? When are you coming back to school? How do you feel?"

"Okay."

"Really?"

"Yeah. Sure."

"You don't sound okay. You sound all limp and draggy. You sound crappy; you don't sound like yourself at all."

I tried to rouse myself, to put energy into my voice. "What does sounding like myself sound like, Jen?" I should have stopped there, but I didn't. Actually, it was as if I couldn't, as if my voice was wound up and couldn't or wouldn't stop until it was completely unwound. "You mean like a normal girl, Jen, like any girl, or like someone whose mother has died? You mean—"

"Silver, stop that."

"—like someone crazed, like someone who wants to scream, like someone who wants to howl. That's me, Jen, that's me. I can howl like a dog or a coyote. I can. I can do it."

I did. I threw my head back and I heard sounds coming out of my throat, sounds I'd never made before, but very like the cries and shrieks I'd heard from the coyotes.

"Sarabeth!" Asa was calling me.

I put my head down, panting.

"It's me, Sarabeth. It's Asa. Jen is crying her eyes out. You scared her. Are you okay? I mean, I know you're not, but why were you doing that?"

"Asa, I don't know. Asa, they're going to cremate my mom. I mean they did it already! The man called, and we're supposed to pick up the . . . the, you know, the ashes; he calls them 'the remains.' So they did it, Asa, they did it."

"But that's good, Sarabeth. We don't have cemetery plots in our family, either. We think it's primitive to dig a hole in the ground and stick a box into it, sometimes even made of concrete, which is completely absurd, because it will never biodegrade. My grandmother is the only one in my family who doesn't agree, but she's so old-world. I wouldn't have it any other way when it's my turn. I want my ashes scattered to the wind and I made out a will saying that."

Asa had made out a will? From pure surprise, for a moment I seemed to come more awake than I had been in days.

"Sarabeth, here's Grant. She wants to talk to you, too. No, wait, Patty first."

"Sarabeth," Patty said, "I just want to tell you we love you, we all love you, and we're waiting for you to come back to school. And Grant wants to play something for you on her flute."

Then I heard Grant's voice. "This is called 'Red Cloud's Song.' Are you sitting down, Sarabeth? Sit down, close your eyes, and listen. All right? Will you do that?"

"Yes," I said, and I did it. I sat down, closed my eyes, kept the phone pressed to my ear, and listened to Grant's flute. It was like listening to a bird singing in a still forest. Mom never liked that really quiet music, but I thought she would have liked this. She would have loved it, and maybe she would have cried, too, listening to it.

The next morning, I got up really early. No more running for the school bus at the bottom of the hill. My school was all the way across the city now, and Cynthia was going to drive me there. We both rushed around getting ready and acting, as Cynthia said, "like chickens with their stupid heads cut off." Because of the morning traffic, it was a thirty-five-minute drive, and she pulled up in front of school exactly two minutes before the last bell.

"Wait for me outside after school," she said. "I'll pick you up. Don't worry if I'm a few minutes late."

"Cynthia." I leaned over and kissed her cheek. "Thank you. Really. I'm sorry I'm such a drag."

"Don't you worry about that. It's not a problem. Just get out there and get going, Sarabeth. That will give me the most satisfaction."

I ran toward the building and up the steps, thinking that Mr. Dunsenay had made an announcement to the whole school about Mom.

Now everyone knew. Suddenly, I panicked at the thought of hundreds of curious eyes peering at me. I turned around to call Cynthia, to tell her I wanted to go back with her, but the VW was already out of sight.

I shouldn't have worried. That morning, it seemed as if half the school hugged me and patted me and told me how sorry they were and that they wanted to help me any way they could. Mrs. Coppel in the office; Mrs. Hilbert, who was my favorite teacher; and even Mr. Abdo, who taught Social Studies and PE, tried to comfort me. And Mr. Dunsenay popped out of his office long enough to squeeze my arm and say, "You just let me know if you need anything."

At lunchtime, my friends were waiting for me at our regular table in the cafeteria. "Here, Sarabeth, sit between me and Grant," Patty said, pulling out a chair.

I sat down and looked around at them. The last time we'd been together in the cafeteria seemed so long ago, but it was actually only five days ago. Then I remembered howling over the phone and I was embarrassed, but none of them mentioned it.

"Where's your lunch?" Jennifer said.

"My lunch?" I looked down as if it should be on the table. "Oh, wow. I must have forgotten it." I'd made a sandwich the night before at Cynthia's urging, but in the rush of getting ready, I hadn't even thought about putting it into my backpack.

"You have to eat, girl," Grant said. She was completely recovered from her flu. "Here, take half my sandwich."

"I have fruit," Asa said, giving me an apple and a handful of dried apricots.

Then they all gave me food, more than I could possibly eat, another half sandwich, celery and carrot sticks, three cookies, and a carton of strawberry yogurt. They took care of me, and not just at lunch, but for the rest of the day, checking up on me in the halls, even wanting to carry my books between classes. "You nuts!" I said. "Stop that. I'm not feeble."

Asa and Jennifer waited outside with me after school for Cynthia. A wind was blowing. Leaves drifted down. "You all are the best," I said. "My mom loved—"

I meant to say "loved you all," but I stopped,

remembering Mom's sneering, "Oh, your friends" on that last morning, as if she had no use for them. It wasn't true. She had been sick that morning. I knew she liked my friends, liked them a lot, approved of them. She had opened her heart and our home to Patty when Patty needed it . . . but still . . . but still, I could hear Mom's voice saying those words. And I wished I couldn't.

"You should have seen Lisa Farger in the locker room after PE," Jennifer said to Asa. "Draping herself all over Silver and crying as if she was Silver's best friend!"

"Lisa's a sympathy monster," Asa agreed. "Anything sad that happens to anyone, that's her meat. If you're suffering, she's in her glory."

Jennifer clicked her tongue disgustedly. "Silver, you should have told that brat to get outta town."

Cynthia pulled up at the curb. She waved to me and called out, "Hi, girls!"

The sun came out as I walked toward the car. It shone through the red leaves of the maples lining the street, and I thought how much Mom had loved seeing the trees change color. She always said fall and spring were her favorite seasons.

And then I thought of that song called "Beautiful Old Life" about all the things that someone who had died would never know again or hear again or see again.

12

The day Cynthia and I were supposed to go to the funeral home, I was so tired and so slow in school that I barely made it on time to any of my classes. "What's the matter?" Patty said when we met for lunch.

"Nothing. Don't feel too great." I opened my lunch bag and then just sat there, looking at it.

"Is everything okay over at Cynthia's?" Grant asked.

I nodded.

"Liar," Jennifer said. She slurped her soda.

"You're pale," Patty said.

"She looks green," Asa said.

Why were they attacking me? Suddenly, I was shaking and my teeth were rattling. Grant got her arm around me, and I tried to pull away, not even knowing what I was doing. My stomach heaved, and I heard Jennifer say, "Uh-oh, I think she's going to toss her cookies."

Then they were all walking me down the hall and into the bathroom, where I threw up what seemed like every meal I'd eaten for a week. They took me to the nurse's office. Blond hair, thin red lips. Questions. More forms to fill out. I tried to make a joke. "The pain police are on the job." I ached everywhere. Eyes, ears, throat, even the hairs on my head ached.

The nurse looked at my tongue and down my throat and in my ears. She took my temperature under my arm. "Someone has to come for you. Who am I to call?"

"Sarabeth has to lie down right now," Asa said in her bossiest manner.

"She will, but I have to call someone for her," the nurse repeated. "She's running a temp."

"Call Cynthia Ramos," I said. I gave the number.

The nurse pointed to a cot in the alcove. "Lie down, Sarabeth. It looks to me like flu. You need rest and lots of liquids. You girls go back to your classes now."

They helped me to the cot. Patty tucked a blanket around me. Jennifer took off my shoes.

"We're going now. We love you, Sarabeth," Grant said.

I love you, too, I said. I wanted to say it,

anyway, and that I would be okay as soon as I was home in my own bed with Tobias on my stomach and Mom in the other room listening to her music. Then a lot of people were talking to me, speaking very fast, like cars racing, and I couldn't understand anything. Then the faces came, changing from one instant to the next, a red face turning into a frowning face turning into a hen's face into a big nose face into a horse's face into . . .

I woke up and thought, I'm really sick. What do I do now? I saw the word SICK dangling in front of my eyes and, then, a little beyond it, I saw Cynthia talking to someone with red lips—oh, the nurse—and knew that I didn't have to think about anything anymore.

"I want to go home," I rasped. I'd been sick for two days. My head seemed to be clamped between metal hands, my arms were concrete, and my legs were spaghetti, but I kept trying to explain to Cynthia that I would take care of myself. I'd been dreaming about it, and I had it all figured out.

"You're talking nonsense. Stop right now." Sitting on the end of the couch, blue eyes flashing points of light, lips drawn back on her teeth,

Cynthia looked demonic to me. I raised my head from the sweaty pillow and tried again to tell her my clever plan to go home and care for myself.

"Shh, shhh. Silly girl, this is fever talk. Here, drink this now; you need lots of liquids." She held a glass of OJ with a straw in it to my mouth. "You don't even know it, but you're being absurd, absolutely absurd."

I sipped the juice, my throat aching with each swallow. Alliteration, I thought, with a great mental effort. Words in a . . . sequence . . . each beginning with . . . the same letter: "absurd, absolutely absurd." Mrs. Hilbert . . . would be . . . proud . . . My eyes closed, and I was asleep again.

Darren stood at the side of the couch and patted my face with his strong little hands. Thump! Thump! "Is that a friendly gesture?" I said, noticing that for the first time in nearly a week, I was speaking a coherent sentence.

Thump! Thump! "Euu Ssabbaa sick," he said. Which I took to mean, "You are sick, Sarabeth."

"Right. And you are healthy, Darren."

Thump! Thump! "Euu Ssabbaa sick," he

communicated again.

"Right. And you're healthy, Darren."

It seemed to me that the two of us were getting along famously, but Cynthia ran in from the kitchen and swooped up Darren. "No, no, baby. Stay away from Sarabeth. Mama doesn't want you to get sick, my big boy. And you shouldn't bother Sarabeth."

"I don't mind, Cynthia. I feel much better today."

"You still need plenty of rest," she said, kissing Darren's neck with loud, juicy kisses that made him giggle. "Want more?" she asked. "Say, 'More kisses, Mama, please.'"

"More kish, pleesh, Mama!"

More kisses came. She dropped him into the swing and gave him a push. "Woooo," he cried, thrusting his legs forward. "Swinin, Mama!"

"Cynthia, when's Billy coming home?" I half sat up. "He hasn't been home all week."

"He should be rolling in here Friday night."

"Did he stay away this week because I'm sick?"

"Partly. He hates it when anyone's sick, he's such a guy about that. But he usually does stay most of the week on the base."

"Do you miss him a lot when he's gone?"

"Sure, but I have my other boyfriend here, don't I?"

She started kissing Darren again on his neck, his fat little arms, his cheeks, his nose. Kisses and love. From the couch, though I could hardly bear to watch, I did. I watched, grinding my teeth, as if my envy was a piece of old dry bread.

13

"That's the way I see it, anyway," Cynthia said. She pushed the dish of spaghetti across the table to me. "Do you take my meaning, Sarabeth? Eat something. Eat some spaghetti at least. You've hardly eaten a thing. I love you to pieces, and I can't bear to see you so skinny!"

"Your meaning about what, Cynthia?" I took a forkful and passed the spaghetti dish on to Billy. I'd been officially over the flu for a week, but I still didn't have much appetite.

"What do you mean, her meaning about *what*?" Billy said, looking at me bright-eyed. He'd come home for the weekend and right away changed out of his uniform into denims and a plaid shirt. "Weren't you listening?" he asked.

"I guess I wasn't listening . . . too well," I said.

"I guess you weren't." He sounded like what he was, a sergeant in the U.S. Army, except he was a supply sergeant, not the kind who screamed at recruits. "How come you weren't listening?"

"I don't know, Billy." I poked at the food on my plate. "I guess my mind just wandered."

"When we're all at the table together, I expect you to be here in mind as well as body."

"Bil-ly," Cynthia said with a downward tilt to her voice. "Come on!"

"No, Cyn, we're a family now. Am I right or not?"

"Yes, of course, but—"

"Am I right, Sarabeth?" He looked at me.

"Yes." It was what he wanted to hear. Anyway, even if we weren't a real family, I thought that we were trying to be one.

"So tell me what you were thinking about so hard that you couldn't listen to what Cynthia was saying."

"I wasn't thinking about much, Billy."

Was telling him my thoughts part of the deal of living with him and Cynthia? I had been thinking about that Thursday morning when Mom was haranguing the radio, remembering how upset she had been. She had said something amusing, though, about bad news and worse . . . worse what? Worse voices? Worse weather? I kept trying to remember what it was that she had said. What that word was. One word, and I couldn't remember it. That was the last morning we were home together. I should remember *everything* about it.

I was thinking other things, too. Thinking that Cynthia used to love me a lot, used to say that if she ever had a child, she hoped it would be a girl just like me. But now she had her son, and she was stuck with me, and it was a toss-up if she even liked me much anymore.

"Let's get on with it," she said. "Sarabeth, I was saying that you getting sick was a message, okay? A wake-up call for you to take care of yourself. You've been stressed-out. No wonder you got the flu, but now you're over it, and it's up to you to keep healthy. You're way too skinny. You lost weight, and look at you, you're hardly eating anything."

"I'm not that hungry tonight, Cynthia."

"This is good food," Billy said.

"Yes, it is, it really is." I tried to sound enthusiastic. "But you know, Cynthia, maybe I was going to get the flu anyway. It was going around.

Grant was sick before Mom—"

I stopped myself. I didn't want to say it, but every thought now was only half a thought, only half-complete, waiting for its tag end: *before Mom died* or *since Mom died*.

We ate for a while in silence. The meatballs passed around once more, and Cynthia got up to check the baby in the bedroom. When she sat down again, she said, "I was just thinking about you being so sick and ranting about living alone, Sarabeth."

"Oh, that." I waved my hand, hoping she wouldn't go into it in front of Billy.

"You should have heard her, Billy. It was actually sort of funny. There's Sarabeth, flat out on her back, saying she's going to live alone and get a job. Right. She's fifteen, running a hundred and three temp, her eyes are bugging out of her head with fever, and she couldn't lift a paper bag if she tried. The perfect employee!"

"But I still sort of wish I could," I said, forking up some green peas.

"You don't like living with us?" Billy said.

"Oh, I do," I said quickly. "It's just, you know,

I miss our place, and—"

"Don't even think it. The Social Services wouldn't let you do it, even if we would," Cynthia said.

"With the Social Services agency in the picture, you don't belong to yourself anymore," Billy said. "I know all about that. They got their hands on me when I was a kid."

"No, Billy, this is different," Cynthia said. "You were in trouble—you were raising hell. That's not Sarabeth. The county's in loco parentis for you now, Sarabeth, which means—"

I knew what it meant.

"—standing in place of parents, which, in turn, means—"

I knew what that meant, too.

"—they get to okay just about everything about you," Billy picked up, "except maybe how many breaths you take in a minute, and they might monitor that, too."

"Billy, it's not that awful," Cynthia said. "They're human beings, and they're overworked, but their intentions are good. Look at how they're letting Sarabeth live with us."

My head went up. "What do you mean, letting me?"

"Well, for you to live with us, we should really have a separate room for you, but the folks there bent the rules. They understand that it's more important for you to live with people you know than with strangers."

"Live with strangers?" My heart suddenly took two loud, shaking beats.

"Actually, yes, they could place you in a foster home. But they didn't—we're your official family."

"Okay," I said.

"That's all?" Billy said. "'Okay'? That's all you're going to say?"

"Uh . . . what?"

"'Uh what?' What kind of talk is that? Is that what they teach you in school?"

"Sorry, but . . . I don't know what you want me to say."

My eyes still hurt—achy achy eyes, that was a song Mom had loved. No, I had it wrong; it was achy achy heart. Wrong again, achy *breaky* . . . heart. That was it. "Achy Breaky Heart." Mom had a record by an old country singer, and whenever she was sad, she played that record, singing along in a quivery, achy breaky voice.

"Sarabeth," Cynthia said. She snapped her fingers. "Are you there? I think Billy wants you to thank me."

"All right," I said, "but for what?" That was a mistake. I should have just said it. Shouted it out. THANK YOU! THANK YOU, CYNTHIA!

"For *what*? How about thinking a little?" Billy said. "Maybe it'll come to you in a big flash of inspiration."

I looked down at my plate. I didn't know what he was talking about, and I didn't know why he was being so sarcastic to me. Get to work, I ordered my achy breaky brain. Give me the answer. I'm supposed to thank Cynthia for, for . . . Brain came through. *For giving you a home.* Oh, right. Because I was an orphan now.

As long as I could remember, I'd been fatherless. Now, I was motherless, too. And I didn't have a home anymore, either. No place that was mine, where I could walk right in and stay and not have to thank people for letting me be there, for letting me sleep on their couch and sit at their table and eat their spaghetti.

Yes, that was it. Now I got it. Thank you, achy breaky brain.

"Thank you, Cynthia," I said.

14

The boy looked up at me. "Hey," he said. His breath puffed out into the cold air. He shaded his eyes from the weak early-morning December sun. "I know you, don't I?"

I nodded.

"Where do I know you from?"

I made a face, hoping it was like Holly Hunter's in that movie where she's a waitress, that little mouth scrunch that says, You don't know? You should!

I was sitting in the top row of the bleachers in the playing field in back of school, huddled inside my coat.

I'd been working on an essay for Mrs. Hilbert when the boy showed up. The moment I saw him, I stopped writing and watched him instead. He walked and then he ran around the snow-packed track, a snail's-pace run, his arms flapping. Not a big-deal runner, but I never took my eyes off him.

It was James.

James, from the school bus I used to ride. James, from algebra class. James, the beautiful brown boy. Dark eyes, big wide mouth, and mass of tight curly hair. And long, long arms and legs. And funny feet. Long and narrow, one going straight, the other turning out at a right angle.

James!

I looked down at him in awe. Right there in front of me, the same James I'd thought about, fantasized about, and once dreamed about as a green bird. What if I told him that?

"Been sitting here long?" he asked.

I made the hand sign, palms up, palms down, and another little mouth scrunch. Yes . . . and no.

"It's early," he said.

I bobbed my head up and down.

"And cold!"

Another head bob.

"I thought I was the only one who got out here this early. It's my thinking time," he added, as if I'd asked.

I tried to look wise, as if I'd figured that out.

"See you, then," he said.

What? He was leaving? "Wait," I said. "Don't go."

He stopped. He stopped because I'd said to! My heart clapped for me. Applause, applause! Or was that shaking of my rib cage, sheer fright and terror?

"So, you do talk. Got anything else to say?"

"Yes, I do."

He put one foot up on the lowest bleacher. "Okay. Shoot."

"I know who you are. You're James Robertson. I know you from two places. From the school bus and from algebra class."

"Aha," he said. "And eureka. So that's how I know you." He climbed toward me, scooping snow into a ball as he moved up the bleachers.

"I have more," I said. "I sit two seats behind you in geometry. Did you ever notice me? No. You used to sit two seats behind me in the bus, so how did you get here so early? That bus never comes this early. I rode it for years, so I know. And another thing," I said, amazing myself with the words pouring out, "that's a wimpy-looking snowball. And what were you talking to yourself about out on the track? And that's it!"

He whistled. "You really do talk. Almost as verbose as me. You say I was talking to myself?" He scooped more snow into the snowball, threw it, and took another step. "Wrong. I wasn't."

"Right. You were."

"So you think I'm weird?"

"No." I could have said a lot more than that, such as, I think you're adorable, I know you're supersmart! You're someone I really want to know, and I can't believe you're talking to me!

The wind whipped his scarf across his face. He was almost up to me now. "Are you absolutely sure I was talking to myself?"

"Yes."

"Okay, I'll tell you what it was about." He sat down next to me. "I was thinking about my sister, and about light, and how I should take her picture in noon light, that perfect shadowless light, so she can't escape being seen."

"I never think about things like that when I take a picture. I guess I should, but—"

"Just put up the old camera and click?" he

said. "That's good, too. Sometimes I need to be more spontaneous, not plan so much. There's a fantastic Japanese photographer, Daido, who runs along the street and snaps pictures as fast as he can, and his photos are actually works of art. Some of them are blurred, too, but it's not like anyone else's blurred; it's as if he planned it. The blurring just adds to the beauty of the picture."

"Did your family live in Japan? Is that how you know about Mr. Daido?" James laughed in a way that embarrassed me. "What?" I said. "What did I say?"

"It's not *Mr.* Daido. That's his first name. Daido Moriyama. My mother read about him—she's a photographer, and she wanted to see his work. Last fall, our whole family took the train down to the city to see the exhibition at the Japan Society. Mom says you could study his pictures for hours and never get bored, and she's right."

"Oh," I said. Why did I say that? I should have said nothing. At least if I'd said nothing, he might be fooled into thinking I was going to come out with some intelligent remark. No wonder he had never noticed me before! He was like a creature from another world, a world of things and ideas I'd never known or thought about, things like Japanese photographers, and taking the train to New York City just to see something, and posing people in noon light.

"Is your sister in our school?" I asked, searching for something to say.

He sat with his elbows on his knees, fists under his chin. "Natalie Robertson, she's a year behind us."

"Is she in Drama Club? Is she going to be in the Christmas play next week? I think I know who she is. Is she really, really pretty?"

"Right, right, right, except this year the play is going to be called a Winter Holiday play, remember? So it doesn't exclude Kwanza and Hanukkah."

"I know. That's cool," I said. "Why do you want to take your sister's picture that way, in noon light?"

"I want light to shine on her, real, natural light. She's something else, you know, special, talented."

"She looks like she is," I said.

"Yeah, she's one of those people, she's got it, but"—he tapped his fists together—"she doesn't know it. She's not showing up yet. So shy. Kind of . . . hiding. Know what I'm saying? I call her my 'artichoke sister.'"

"You mean, like, the layers?"

"Right. All there, only you can't see what's under them."

"You like her a lot," I said.

"Well . . . yeah. She's my sister. Also happens to be one of my favorite people in the world."

I fell silent, wondering what it must be like to have a brother. Not just any brother, either, but one who adored you.

"And what about you?" he said. "Who are you?"

"Oh . . . me. I'm Sarabeth Silver."

"Little white girl, is that all you can say? Your name? Are you another artichoke child? Say something else. Tell me more," he demanded.

I stared at him, thick-tongued, my snowball heart crunching inside me. "Not much to tell," I managed to say. "No sisters. No broth—"

Then the bell rang, and we both stood up. I went down the risers next to him, in step with him, and once he reached out to keep me from slipping on a snow-slick place, and all that seemed like enough happiness for one day and, really, more than enough.

❧

15

Saturday morning, before I was out of bed, Billy was in the living room working out. Lying on the couch, the covers half over my head, I listened to him counting off push-ups. A few days before, Cynthia and I had turned the couch around so that it faced the wall. "From here to the wall, this space is yours," Cynthia said, her hands on the back of the couch. "Now you have a room of your own." She made a little face. "Well, sort of. I wish it was a lot better."

"No, it's great," I said. "Thank you."

Billy wasn't happy about the change. This had been his couch, his place to have a beer, read the paper, and watch TV. It had been his I'm-not-an-army-man-now-just-a-regular-guy place.

"Me, I get to sit there by invitation only," Cynthia used to joke. Now nobody got to sit there or sleep there or sprawl there except me. It was my place. I did everything there. Listened to music, read, did homework there—when I did it. I kept all my private things in that space, close by me.

"Billy!" Cynthia yelled from the bedroom.

"What?" He was running in place now.

"Do you have to do that?"

"Yes, I do." He ran harder, pounded louder.

He was home for the weekend. The first thing he always did was change from army fatigues into jeans and an old shirt. The next thing was pick up Darren and throw him in the air a few dozen times. I always liked Billy most when he played with the baby.

"Billy, please stop!" Cynthia called. "That's driving me mad, and probably all our neighbors, too."

He kept on jumping around, and I lay there waiting for him to leave so I could get up, and thinking of Mom, little bits of memory.

Something smelled really good. Mom, are you actually cooking? I said, but the windows were rattling, and she was worried that it was a storm. I'll see, I said. Then my eyes opened, and I sat up, surprised that I'd slept.

Cynthia appeared, carrying Darren in his pj's. "Billy!"

Billy stopped running and wiped his face with a towel. "Cyn, what's the problem?"

I slipped down under the blankets again while they argued. Finally Billy went off to take a shower, and Cynthia carried Darren into the kitchen. I got up and folded my blankets. While I was digging around for clothes, Billy came out of the shower, wrapped in a towel.

"Get dressed, will you please," Cynthia said. She was hanging Darren's laundry on a rack over the heating vent. "Don't go around like that! Anyway, I want to go out for a walk, so you need to watch Darren."

"How long are you going to be gone?" Billy said. "I have a pool game with Mark."

"I'll watch the baby, Cynthia," I said on my way to take a shower.

Cynthia didn't answer. Not a surprise. She hardly let me do anything for Darren. Mom and I had noticed her possessiveness with him a long time ago, and we'd talked about it. Mom's theory had been that Cynthia was overprotective of the baby because it had taken her so many years to get pregnant.

"She said she'll watch Darren," Billy said to

Cynthia. *She*—that was me. In the weeks that I'd been living with him and Cynthia, he'd almost stopped calling me by my name.

Before I even got the bathroom door shut, I heard them arguing again. I was hoping it would be over by the time I was dressed, but as I came out of the bathroom, I heard Cynthia yelling, "This is a mess! A mess!"

Did she mean the kitchen? Maybe. Maybe not. Her bedroom was a mess, too. The whole place was pretty much a mess, no matter how hard we tried to keep it neat. There was another kind of mess, too, mornings when she drove me to school—the mess of us rushing to get dressed, and get the baby ready, and all of us downstairs and into the car. Some mornings, Cynthia didn't make it out of her pj's, just pulled on a jacket and went out.

The day before had been one of those mornings, only worse. She ran out barefoot, Darren in her arms. "I'll go back for your shoes," I said. There was snow on the ground. But she told me not to bother and barefooted the gas pedal all the way across town.

Later that day, Cynthia and Billy made up

their quarrel and went out together with the baby. "We'll be awhile," Cynthia said. "Why don't you call one of your friends? Don't hang around alone."

"I won't," I said. I didn't tell her that I knew everyone was busy this weekend. Asa's parents were having a family party, Grant had gone away the night before with her mother and stepfather to ski in Vermont, Jen had to baby-sit about a dozen of her little siblings—actually, only two of them—and Patty had said something about visiting a cousin in Connecticut.

Patty had been a little vague, though, so I called her and got lucky. She answered the phone. "You're home!" I said.

"Yes, I am. We didn't go. Want to do something? Want to meet at the mall? I need to get out of here. You'd be doing me a big favor."

We agreed to meet in an hour. I went right out to catch a bus. A bulky woman carrying a shopping bag sat down next to me. She was panting, that kind of wheezy breathing that comes from years of smoking.

"You shouldn't slump like that, dear," she wheezed, pouring hot cigarette breath over me.

I nodded. I'd learned in these past weeks that if I didn't want to talk, I didn't have to. All I had to do was nod, and most people were satisfied.

"Try not to look so all-around droopy," the woman said. "Try to have a more peppy-looking face; you'll have more friends."

I nodded again, thinking that if advice was money, I'd be rich. If it was food, I'd be fat. If it was beauty, hands down I'd be Miss Teenage America.

It seemed as if everyone I knew, plus 90 percent of their relatives, had taken turns giving me advice about grieving, getting over grief, getting healthy, getting with it, and getting on with my life. I'd been told I needed quiet and stimulation, company and solitude, exercise and sleep, vitamins C, A, and E, echinacea—whatever that was—deep breathing, tai chi, jogging, guts, and courage. Lots of courage. And talk. Lots of talk. I'd been told that time would heal my heart, that all wounds eventually closed, and someday all this would seem like a bad dream.

It was a shopping list for grief. Take three with aspirin. I wasn't surprised when teachers and friends gave me advice, or even friends of friends, but when strangers started pitching in, it made me wonder if there was a sign on my forehead begging for advice that everyone could see, except me.

"And now I'm going to tell you something else," the woman wheezed.

I knew she was going to do that.

"Whatsoever is bothering you—and don't say nothing, because I know there is; I've got that quality of seeing into somebody's head—whatsoever, I say, do it your own way." Then, maybe to make sure I was taking this in properly, she pinched my arm hard.

When I met Patty and told her about the woman on the bus, she laughed. "It's always easy to tell other people things. Don't let it throw you, Sarabeth."

We shopped for a while. Patty bought socks and a few other things; then we went into the bookstore. Patty plucked a book off the NEW ARRIVALS shelf. "I saw this guy on TV the other night. He's so funny. He could probably make even my stepfather laugh."

"He has confidence in himself, I bet." I was

thinking about that woman, how she'd given me advice with complete assurance that she was right and should tell me what she thought. "Where do you get confidence like that?" I said to Patty. "Like this guy on TV? Like the woman on the bus? Okay, he's got talent, but what about her? I would never have the confidence to tell a stranger how to live her life. I wouldn't dream of doing that."

"That's because you're a rational being, Sarabeth."

"And that's a complete illusion, Patty." We wandered through the bookstore aisles. "You always make me sound better than I am. If confidence was for sale, hey, I'd be first in line. I could use a bucketful, but I'd settle for even a pinch."

"You're doing it again," Patty said, stopping at the poetry section. "Putting yourself down." She took a book off the shelf and turned it over to show me a picture of the author.

I looked over her shoulder. For once, Patty was wrong. I wasn't putting myself down. I *had* lost my confidence. There was nothing that I was sure about, nothing I knew absolutely, anymore.

Well, no, there was one thing. I knew I wanted Mom back. That was it, the sum of everything I was clear about. Everything else in my life was just muddle and confusion.

16

To get to Travisino's office in the Veterans Hospital, which I didn't want to get to, never wanted to get to, but was obliged to get to, I took two buses up to Trowbridge Hospital on Seneca Road. If Travisino's office had been any-where else, I might not have hated going there so much.

Nothing had changed since the day Chester Jay drove me there six weeks earlier. There was the same big green sign, TROWBRIDGE HOSPITAL, and the same maple trees lining the same snow-spattered road. And there was the same looming brick building and the same door I'd walked through. And if I went inside, I could find the same room where I'd seen the little lump of Mom in the bed, only someone else would be in it now.

The Vets Hospital was on a road behind Trowbridge. Listening to Chester Jay, I'd had the idea that it was some great place. Maybe for him. I entered a back door opening into a dim corri-dor that always smelled faintly of soggy garbage.

I took an elevator to the third floor, walked down a long hall, opened Travisino's door, and looked in.

"Sarabeth! Come on in!" He always acted happy to see me, as if he were my uncle and not my social worker. "Sit down. Tell me something," he said. "Let's talk! How was your week?"

"Okay. Why is your office so cold?"

"It's cold outside, and this is an old building." Then he got down to business, which, according to him, was to guide me through "the grieving process." Which sounded like some sort of long dark tunnel. And maybe it was. "Last time you were here, we were talking about ways of knowing things," he said. "Remember?"

"Yes."

"In the head and in the belly. And we were saying the belly is the real place of feeling, and not the heart, like people always say."

"Yeah, yeah," I said, walking around the office. "Only *we* weren't saying it. You were saying it."

"Human beings get trapped in their minds; they construct ideas and fit their emotions into the ideas. But real things happen, which is called 'experiential knowledge,' and from this kind of knowledge, we construct, if we're healthy, other modes of thought."

Listening to Travisino talk this way was like being trapped in mud. Pull out one foot and the other foot sucks you down even deeper. But I couldn't help thinking that it was too bad I couldn't bring some of these words home to Mom. She'd love *experiential*. She was a sucker for big words. "College word," she'd say gleefully, and she'd scribble it on a scrap of paper and throw it in a drawer with the other scraps with words like *dour* and *voracious* and *multitudinous*.

I looked out the window at the piles of snow. The last time I'd been here, Travisino had worked me over with tough love, and he went at it again. "Sarabeth, this 'Yeah, yeah' stuff is telling me you're depressed, you're mad, really mad."

"I'm not!"

"And we both know why. You're mad at your mother for dying. Simple as that. Listen, you can admit it. Nobody'll put you in jail for being angry about her deserting you."

"Deserting me?" I rapped my knuckles against the cold window. "That's what you call what happened to my mother?"

"She dumped you; she left you alone in the world." He kept at it until, just to shut him up, I said what he wanted to hear.

"Okay, you're right, I'm mad at her. I'm insanely furious. Is that better? Do you feel better now?"

"You're the one who's going to feel better," he said, swiveling in his chair. "You're speaking truth; these are natural feelings. Why shouldn't you feel mad? She should have taken better care of herself. She should have gone to a doctor when she felt so crummy. She should have—"

"We didn't have the money for a doctor. Don't you know anything, you stupid man!" I leaned my forehead against the window, wishing I could push through the glass, just spread my arms and go . . . somewhere. Anywhere.

The night before, late, Darren had been crying, and I'd heard Cynthia soothing him back to sleep. "Sssh, little bear, little sweetheart, little darling, Mama's precious. Sssh, little one, go to sleep," she sang, "little most beautiful baby in the world, little sweetheart, Mama's precious, pretty darling." In the darkness, I had listened to every word of love and hated it. It was awful how much

I'd hated it, awful to be jealous of a baby.

Now Travisino was talking about dreams and how they could help us understand ourselves. I tried not to listen. Did he think I was going to tell him about my dreams? Never. Dreams in which I kicked and hit people, punched walls, and wailed as if my heart was breaking all over again. The next day, I was always tired from one of these dreams.

I'd been tired all day today, and now I was trembling, and I heard myself saying, "You're right, it was crappy of Mom to die. She shouldn't have done it; she shouldn't have left me! No, she shouldn't have!"

I hated Travisino for getting me to crack like that, but he was nearly ecstatic over it. "That's a breakthrough, Sarabeth! That's great! You're going to feel so much better after this."

"Oh right, just *great*," I said, trying to get back the cool, sarcastic tone. I sat and draped one leg over the arm of the chair. "Maybe we're both certifiable." He leaned across the desk, looking interested. "Your saying I should be mad at her—that's crazy. And me agreeing—even crazier. As if she planned her death, did it like any chore."

He started explaining that his saying Mom deserted me was a metaphor for an emotion, that we both knew it wasn't logical and I didn't have to be ashamed of my feelings, et cetera, et cetera. I wasn't listening. I was thinking that the truth was that I could see Mom making a plan, saying to herself, Time to die, Jane, and then congratulating herself on a job well done and thinking, That should teach that daughter of mine something about real life.

She was always so afraid I'd repeat her life, get swept away by bad luck, bad timing, or bad choices. But I was me, not her. More and more, it had irritated me the way she hovered over me.

You don't have that problem anymore, so quit whining.

Mom, quit butting in, I'm just stating the facts. You could be a pain, and you know it.

It was for your own good. Look at the way you're talking. I didn't bring you up to be a smart aleck!

The word is diss, Mom, and if you don't like it, stop hanging around me. Go away and be dead. Leave me alone!

"What?" Travisino said. "What'd you say, Sarabeth?"

I shrugged and put on a smile. "I was telling Mom to get out of my head and be dead." I couldn't hold the smile. I wanted those words back. Tears welled in my eyes. Travisino reached across his desk and, for once, he didn't say anything, just patted my hand.

17

"We came over to get some things for Sarabeth from her house and figure out what we're going to do with the rest," Leo said to Dolly Krall, "but there's a lock on the door over there, and we can't get in."

"That's right," she said. "How are you, Sarabeth?"

"Okay," I said. "How about you?"

"Me, I'm always good." She was standing in her doorway, filling it with her bulk. "I'm having the place painted, and I don't want any old anyone going in there, so I locked it up."

"Painted," I said, and before I could stop myself, I added stupidly, "You're doing that for us?"

"No, honey, not for you. There ain't any more *us*, remember? Your mom's gone. You're not living there anymore. You haven't been there for weeks. I've got it rented out to real nice people. They're paying for a new kitchen floor themselves, right out of their own pocket. Soon as it's done, they're moving in."

"You rented the place?" Leo blew on his hands. We were deep in a cold snap, and he'd left his gloves in the truck. "I thought Jane was paid up a month ahead, right to the end of the year."

"What are you saying?" Dolly asked.

"Renting the place when it's still legally Sarabeth's, that's not exactly kosher," Leo said.

Dolly's hands snapped onto her hips. "The circumstances, sir! I got people wanting to move in, I ain't turning customers away. I'm a business-woman. And here's something else: I didn't get a month's notice from anyone. And you talk about legal," she ended disgustedly.

"And what are you saying, Mrs. Krall? Jane was supposed to give you a month's notice before she had the heart attack?"

"Don't get smart with me," Dolly said. She looked as if she was ready to pick up Leo and shake him.

"So Sarabeth has a refund coming, I guess," Leo said.

"Are you joking? The condition that place was in? Had to be painted from head to toe. A door had to be replaced, plus some tiles in the bathroom. Let me tell you, I'll give you an itemized bill and you can see for yourself."

"Good!" Leo said.

"What about our stuff?" I said. "Mom's stuff. Where is it?"

"We took care of it. Don't you worry about that," Dolly said. "Fred and me did it together. We got it all stored, waiting for you, and why don't you get that sour look off of your face, Sarabeth. You think we want your things? Fred and me got a lot nicer stuff than you and your mom ever had, no offense meant."

She crooked her finger at me. "Come on in, take a load off. You, too," she said to Leo. "I'll put on my boots and walk you over to the storage shed. You can see everything for yourselves."

"That's okay; we'll wait out here," Leo said.

"Suit yourself." Dolly let the door slam behind her.

"Jeeze, oh man, she's a piece of work," Leo said. He blew on his hands again. "I'm going to get my gloves. You warm enough? You're not wearing a hat. I've got an extra in the truck."

"No, I'm okay," I said, but I was cold, and I followed him to the truck. This morning, I'd had a brainstorm and called to ask if he'd bring Tobias along, so I could have a visit. Now I climbed into the front seat and picked him up.

"You're beautiful again," I said, holding Tobias up to my face. "Do you know me? Have you forgotten me? You better not!" Leo had left the engine running, so the truck was warm. I kissed Tobias's nose, his ears, and each of his paws. He furled and unfurled his claws, his eyes half-closed.

Dolly came out of her house, wearing a red hunting jacket and black rubber boots. "Yoo hoo!" she called.

I put Tobias down, and Leo and I followed Dolly through the trailer park, way to the back, past the rows of homes. At the end of the last row, the one closest to the sheared-off cliff behind the court, she stopped in front of a rusting silver trailer.

"I saved you a lot of work, Sarabeth, in case you don't know it," she said, unlocking the door. "That was no little easy moving job that Fred and I did. Those beds alone were killers."

She held the door open. "Look around, get whatever you want. Take your time."

It was colder inside than out—cold, damp, and dim. All I could see at first was a clutter of lumpy shapes. Then Mom's bureau, with a couple of kitchen chairs on top of it, came clear. After that, everything. My bed frame, the old rocker, lamps, chairs, mattresses on end, and boxes and plastic bags heaped everywhere. I'd seen this storage trailer so many times before, but I'd never thought about it, never wondered who used it or what was in it. Now I knew. We were in it. Mom and me.

"Where's that red couch?" Leo said. "The love seat?"

"Oh, that thing." Dolly was half in, half out, holding the door open. "Fred and I put it in our place, so as it wouldn't get ruined here." She shifted, and her shadow fell over Leo. Behind her, the sun was going down behind the cliff.

"Well, hey," Leo said, crossing his arms. "I think we just want that couch back in here. Don't we, Sarabeth? And what else, Mrs. Krall? Anything else missing from here?"

"There's nothing missing from here. Don't start with me, fella. That moth-eaten couch isn't missing; there's nothing missing or illegal here.

You should be thanking me, not mouthing off at me."

"You'll bring the couch back here then, until Sarabeth decides what to do with it, right?" Leo turned his back on her. "Sarabeth, what are we looking for?" He propped the door open with a chair. "We'll let you know when we're done," he said to Dolly.

"You do that!" She went down the stairs, making a lot of noise with her boots.

I watched her walk away, stomping her feet into the snow. "Thanks, Leo."

"What for? Don't tell me. I know. I got rid of the dragon lady."

"Not just that." I knelt and opened a box. The toaster was in it and newspaper-wrapped plates and glasses with a bunch of Mom's scarves stuffed in at the sides, the ones she wore over her hair when she worked. I put her favorite scarf, a white one with yellow fish, in my backpack, then pulled the tape off another box. This one was filled with shoes and boots.

"I mean thanks for everything," I said to Leo. "The couch and, you know, everything. Driving me here. You didn't have to do that."

"Come on," he said, "it's nothing. Don't embarrass me. We've been friends for a long time, you and me."

"You and Mom," I said.

"The three of us were friends," Leo said. He looked at me. "The three of us. Okay?"

"Sure," I said, shrugging.

Leo sighed. "So, what are you wanting to find here? Give me a clue, Sarabeth. I'll start looking, too."

I closed up the boot box and put it to one side. "Do you remember my old quilt, the one with rabbits on it?"

"Rabbits? Really?"

"Yeah, bunny wabbits. It was my baby quilt. You could look for that." There were a few other things I wanted, nothing big. Mom's gold sun catcher, a hairbrush I was missing, some of my clothes. "You gave me a book of cat cartoons for my birthday a couple of years ago. I'd like that."

"Send it back with me, so Tobias can have a laugh."

"Cute," I said. I was looking into a black plastic garbage bag. Utensils, shampoo, cookbooks, clothes. "Is Tobias okay?" I asked. "Is it working out all right for him to live with you?"

"It's working out great. He and Pepper really clicked. He gets big-time attention from her."

"He does?" I said. "What if he forgets me?"

"He's never going to forget you. You're his mom."

I opened another box, then another. I rearranged stuff, picking up things that had been Mom's and putting them back carefully. "Leo, here's that garlic press you gave us."

"Did you guys ever use it?"

"Not me. Mom was the garlic lover."

Way at the bottom of a box, I found a small address book with a faded blue cover. Most of it was filled with names of neighbors and the people Mom had worked for. Next to some names, she'd drawn little symbols—a question mark, a frowny face, an exclamation point. In the back of the notebook under "Hinchville" was a handful of names and phone numbers. Doreen and Thomas Halley—555-3311. Netta Bishop—555-3090. Elizabeth Wardly—555-4466. Judith and Martin Silver—555-6085. Doreen and Thomas Halley were Mom's parents, that much

I knew. The other names didn't mean anything to me.

"Sarabeth." Leo looked up from a box he was pawing through. "I found the sun catcher."

"Great. Leo, did you know Mom put a heart next to your name in her address book?"

He knelt down and took the notebook. "Oh man . . ." He gave a kind of whimpering laugh. "She was the one who deserved it, not me. She had the big heart."

I reached over and flipped to the Hinchville page. "Look at this."

"Yeah, I know. I think your mom always believed that someday she'd pick up the phone and someone from her family would be on the line, her mother or—"

"Her mother, my so-called grandmother? I don't think so." My heart seemed to speed up and beat very hard. I wrapped my arms around my knees. "I hate those people, Leo. I really hate them."

Leo took my chin in his hand, but I pulled away. "Don't go there, Sarabeth," he said. "I'm telling you, don't go to that place where you hate people. Your mom never did."

"Yoo hoo." Dolly was back, filling the doorway. "Sarabeth, forgot to say that you can leave your stuff sit here for another week, max; then you got to get it out or pay storage. Whichever, is okay with me. I'll charge you less than those big rip-off storage companies, anyway."

I stood and dusted off my jeans. "Okay," I said.

"Okay, you want to do it?"

"I don't know." I put Mom's address book in my pocket. "I have to think about it."

She shrugged. "Suit yourself." She was gone again, stamping down the steps.

"Leo, what do you think? What do I do with all our stuff? I can't bring anything over to Cynthia's. There's no room there."

"We'll figure it out," he said. "I think we should store it someplace better than this, one of those metal sheds where you know it won't get water-damaged or anything."

"Can I afford it?"

"Don't worry about it. If you can't, I'll take care of it. Not a big deal."

We didn't find the book of cat cartoons, but when we left, I had my quilt, the sun catcher, the address book, and a framed photo that Mom had always kept on her bureau, a studio shot of her and my father. It was their wedding picture, just the two of them—no family. My father was wearing a suit and a tie, and Mom was wearing a dress, her hair cut short and draped over one side of her forehead. They were sitting next to each other, their heads touching, very serious. No fake "take my picture" smiles. Just their real faces looking out at me. Cynthia always said I looked like Mom, but Leo said I looked like my father. Half and half, I always thought.

In the truck, I put Tobias on my lap and took the picture out of my backpack to look at it again. I noticed that the glass was cracked across one edge. "It wasn't cracked before, when Mom had it," I said to Leo. "It must have happened when Dolly and Fred packed up our stuff."

I held the picture up to the light. Mom's dress was red and close-fitting, almost a twin to the one she'd worn the night we ran through Roadview holding hands and looking for the rain. Mom had been a teenager when the picture was taken, and pregnant. So, really, I was in it, too. The three of us, our family, we were all in it together. I kissed the picture. "You guys were so brave," I said.

18

❧

"Dolly Krall just *loomed* in the doorway," I said, looking around the table at my friends. We were in the Waffle Iron, sharing one of their "extraordinary superstrawberry waffles," and while we ate, I was making a story—a good one, I hoped—out of Leo's and my foray to the storage trailer.

"Dolly filled that whole space. She was steaming! You could practically see it coming out of her ears."

Remembering that Mrs. Hilbert had said good storytelling was detailed, I stuffed in as many details as I could remember. The black garbage bags tumbled every which way, Leo going mano a mano with Dolly over her renting the trailer, the chairs perched on the bureau, the cracked glass in my parents' picture, and Leo's almost crying when he saw the heart near his name in Mom's address book.

I even mentioned the fish scarf, which I planned to keep with me all the time now. "Here it is," I said, taking the scarf out of my backpack.

"How cute!" Jen said.

"I love it," Asa said, and she reached for it.

"No, no, no. No touch." I put the scarf back in my backpack and kept talking. I was talking a lot, telling them the whole story of that afternoon.

No, not really. I fudged it. I left out stuff. I left out my sadness. I knew what I was doing. Pretending to be so okay. Normal. No more long face. I made my eyes big. I talked fast. I made it all as funny as I could. I even made Dolly funny, someone you could laugh at, someone you could laugh off.

"You could probably go on the stage, Sarabeth," Asa said. "You could be one of those people who make their lives into a show. A one-woman show. The story of your life, with chapters. This one would be called 'Dearest Dolly.'"

Jennifer, always having to go Asa one better, said, "I'd call it 'The Dolly Krall Kommando Raid.'" Then we all started making up chapter titles, the sillier the better, for different parts of our lives. It was the first time I'd really laughed since Mom died.

I took to carrying around Mom's address book in my back pocket, maybe because it was the only thing I had in her handwriting. We'd never been separated long enough to write letters. Saturday, when Cynthia and I were in the park with Darren, taking turns pushing him on the swing, I showed her the address book. I pointed out her name with stars around it, and then I showed her the page with Mom's relatives, the Hinchville people.

"That kills me," she said. "Her keeping those names all these years."

"Leo says Mom never stopped thinking someone would get in touch with her someday."

"She should have ripped those names out and burned them. I would have! Such *nice* people, those Halleys. Open them up, and, what do you bet, you'd find gravel where their hearts ought to be. Your mom and dad were just kids. So they rushed things—so what!" She narrowed her eyes at me. "Think how hurt she must have been! Her own mother kicking her out."

Cynthia lit a cigarette and gave Darren another push. "And then not even out of her teens, and she's on her own with you. But she never lost heart, never threw herself around and bawled, like someone else might have."

Someone else. That meant me, didn't it?

The cigarette hung on the edge of her lip. The wind picked up the smoke and blew it toward Darren. "Don't you worry about secondhand smoke?" I said.

Did she even hear me? She waved her hand in the air, maybe to brush me off, maybe to push away the smoke. Maybe both.

"Jane never felt sorry for herself," she mused. "She was so tough. If she'd lived, she would have been one of these tough old ladies—you know the type, tough old birds. She was a trouper, a fighter." Cynthia looked up. A mist of clouds traveled in a high wind across the sky. "God, I miss that woman," she said. She crossed her arms over her chest and stood there, smoking and staring up at the clouds.

I gave Darren a push.

And what about you, Sarabeth?

What about me? Push.

Are you a fighter?

I don't know. Push.

Are you a trouper?

I don't know. Push.

Are you tough?

I don't know. Push. I don't know. Push. I. Don't. Know. Push. Push. Push.

Push until arms ache.

Push until Darren's feet hit the sky.

Push until he screams with pleasure and Cynthia screams with anger. "What the hell are you doing? He's too high. Stop that, Sarabeth! Stop!"

Then walk away to the fence, grip the metal diamondwork, look at the clouds wavering across the sky, and wait until the trembling stops.

19

⚛

"**I**s the box with your mom's ashes really under the couch where you sleep?" Grant asked. She was sitting behind me on the bed, braiding my hair.

"Yes, it's there," I said.

"What does it look like?" Jen asked.

"Like a regular square white cardboard box, about the size of a cake box. Weighs about the same, too. Any other questions?"

It was New Year's Eve, and we were all in Grant's bedroom, in our pj's, or what passed for pj's, Jen in footy pajamas, the kind little kids wore, the rest of us in T-shirts and sweatpants. We'd had a little supper and a lot of dessert, including a double-chocolate cake that Grant's mom had bought at the best bakery in the city. We were planning to stay up until at least midnight, but probably later, to see in the New Year.

Asa raised her soda can. "A toast to mom-in-a-box. Here's to her."

"Asa!" Grant and Patty spoke at the same time.

Asa's face reddened. "I'm just trying to make Sarabeth laugh."

"So when you got the box from the funeral home," Jen said, "where'd you put it in the car?"

"I held it in my lap. And I opened it and looked inside."

Jen shuddered. "You didn't."

"What's the big deal, Jen? It's not her mom in there," Asa said. "It's just ashes. What do they look like, Sarabeth?"

"Asa!" Grant and Patty said again.

"They're gray, Asa," I said, "and there's bits of hard white stuff mixed in. Bone."

"Wow," Patty said. "That's . . . I really think that's spiritual. Don't you think so? Don't you think there's something of your mom in there, Sarabeth? I mean her essence, her spirit."

I nodded. I had thought the same thing. It was really why I didn't mind having the box under the couch.

"Cynthia wanted me to give the box to Leo to keep," I said. "She thought having it in the apartment would upset me. She was ready to go right over to Leo's after we left the funeral home. She said if no one was there, we could leave it in the mailbox."

"She didn't say that," Grant said. "Tell me she didn't say the mailbox. That sounds like something Asa would say."

"I bet Leo's girlfriend, Pepperandsalt, would have really wanted your mom's ashes in her mailbox," Jen said.

They finally changed the topic when Jen decided to make up Asa's face. "I know you hate makeup, but let's just give it a whirl," Jen said. We all began making up one another and talking about boys. For the first time in years, probably since kindergarten, Jen said, she didn't have a secret love, a passionate crush, or even a so-so boyfriend-on-a-string thing going.

"Now I'm really worrying about Jen even more than about Sarabeth," Patty said.

Which could have been my cue to say something about James, not necessarily to confess my crush, but just to mention him casually as someone I liked and thought maybe liked me back. I could have told them about talking to him in geometry, lending him paper one day, his lending me a pen another day, and both of us saying hi in the halls—big smiles—whenever we passed each other.

But I wasn't really thinking about James. Cynthia was on my mind and had been lingering there since two nights ago when I overheard her on the phone talking to someone about me and Mom.

I smoothed light green eye shadow on Patty's eyelid. "Hold still, Patty." My voice caught. "Cynthia said we were a '*tragedy.*'" I lilted my voice, trying to catch Cynthia's operatic tones. "'*Un*believable. You would not *think* such a thing could happen *again*. Ten years ago, a *mere* ten years, her father was in a *freak* accident.' She's gossiping about my life! What is it to her, just a story, like a play where she aced the lead, got the great part!"

Asa was staring at me with a dumbfounded expression, and I thought, If I keep on like this, they will all despise me. Yet, I couldn't seem to stop.

"She gets to be *sooo* sad and *sooo* sympathetic. She took in the orphan child; isn't she just *sooo* good?"

Patty and Grant exchanged looks, and my

heart took a huge lunge. I told myself to simmer down. I knew that what I was saying was unfair. I remembered Patty's telling me once that I was an "even" person, meaning I didn't let things get to me, meaning I didn't rant and rave. Maybe I'd been that person before Mom died, but no more. I was jagged now; I had sharp edges. I was righteous, too, ready to shout through the fire in my heart at anyone who crossed my path. *Do you know how lucky you are, or are you too stupid to know?*

I didn't like me much anymore, and I didn't see why anyone else should, either. James . . . well, he was just a little miracle. But he didn't really know me, and who knew how long that would last.

"She cried," I said. "Cynthia cried on the phone. You know how I hate that? I don't want to hear her crying over me or Mom."

"She was your mom's best friend," Grant said. "She's got a right, Sarabeth."

"You can say that, Grant, but I've heard enough crying to last me the rest of my life. Enough 'Poor Sarabeth,' 'Oh, Sarabeth.' I know what everyone's going to say before they even think it. Am I okay, and how am I, really? And their soppy voices and how any moment I'll feel better. And I don't want to hear how proud everyone is of me for taking things so well. Oh, yes, I take things so well. You can see how great I'm doing!"

I twirled Patty around in the chair. "I'm done!" I dropped onto the bed and covered my eyes with my hand. "Sorry," I said. "I blew it. Sorry, you shouldn't have to listen to me doing that. . . . If my mom came back tonight, do you think she'd even recognize me?"

"Are you kidding, girl?" Jen said. "Your own mother?"

"I've changed, Jen. I'm not a nice person anymore. You can all see that. Sometimes I don't even recognize myself. It's like I'm a house that a stranger has moved into and taken over. I'm not the person Mom wanted me to be. I'm mean; I'm rude and smug—"

"Stop that," Patty said. "Stop putting yourself down."

"If you could see into my heart, you'd know I'm just telling the truth."

"Sarabeth," Grant said. She sat next to me and stroked my hair. "You're the same person you always were."

I hid my face in my hands. Why did they have to be kind to me? I didn't want it; it made me too ashamed. I couldn't even tell them the truth, that sometimes I loved them the way I always had, but sometimes I hated them, hated how much they had and how little I had.

"Sarabeth," Grant said again.

"I'm sorry. It's being without Mom that makes me crazy."

"I'd be crazy, too, without my mom," Jen said.

"It's like doing really hard work," I said. "You feel tired all the time. Sometimes, just breathing is hard. Being without Mom has changed everything. It's confusing, and maybe that's the hardest part of it all. Or, I don't know, the really hard part could be just thinking about her."

"Running the mom movies?" Asa said.

"Yes." I half laughed. "Sometimes they're really cool and I like it; I like remembering stuff about her. She could be so funny." I started crying.

Grant started crying, too, and then so did Patty. It was contagious. Jen was next. Asa held out for about five seconds, and then she joined in, and we were all crying and holding on to one another. They were crying for me, but for themselves, too. I knew it. They all had things to cry over, even if, most of the time, they never talked about it.

It was midnight, and we didn't even realize it. We had planned to toast one another with grape coolers, but instead we cried our way into the New Year.

20

※

"**D**o what?" I said to Billy.

"Has she got hearing problems?" Billy looked across the table at Cynthia with a little smile. Smile said, Can't she take a joke? He had a bunch of jokes like that. "Has she got speech problems?" "Does she ever say anything?" "Is she of any use around here?"

"You want me to do what, Billy?" I said again.

"Transfer," he said. "To Hugo Everts, which is the school nearest to where you live now. Which is *here*." With each word, the toothpick he was chewing on bounced on his lip. "Cyn's been running you all the way across the city every morning for weeks, and then picking you up every afternoon. That is way too much. And as it's a new year and a new term, I thought it would be appropriate to have a nice fresh start."

"It isn't every day," I said. "I try to keep it down. I don't like Cynthia driving me all the time, either. That last week, before vacation? I took the bus three mornings—"

"I don't care if you were getting up four mornings out of five, which you weren't," Billy said. "I don't want Cynthia to have that responsibility. I don't want her doing that anymore, period. Okay? She's not going to do that, plus the baby and everything else."

I took an orange from the bowl in the middle of the table and squeezed it between my hands. "Billy, okay, I understand, but I don't want to transfer schools. I can't! I mean, I like my school. I like my teachers. I—"

"You'll like these teachers, too. Why not? You'll have a new experience. It'll be good for you, I guarantee you that."

"But all my friends are over there—"

"Are they going to stop being your friends because you're at another school? If they do, they're not the kind of people you want for friends. Am I right? Come on, answer me, am I right?"

I dug my thumbnail into the skin of the orange. "I guess so."

"You guess right. Hugo Everts is four blocks away. You can roll out of bed and be there in five minutes. I'll tell you something else. Now is the time, before the term really gets under way. Hugo

Everts is a good school—no problem there, we checked it out." He looked over at Cynthia. "Tell her, Cyn."

"He's right. It *is* a good school; we checked it out," Cynthia said.

Our eyes met. She was steady in her glance, letting me know that she agreed with Billy. That she wanted me to do this. Wanted me to change schools. Didn't want to drive me back and forth across the city anymore. And I couldn't blame her for that. I don't know if even Mom would have been as good about doing that as Cynthia had been for so many weeks.

"Think about this," Billy said. "You can sleep another hour every morning, maybe two. I always wanted to sleep more when I was your age."

"Can't you see him, Sarabeth, snoozing away?" Cynthia tapped my arm, giving me a smile that asked for one in return. "His poor mom—trying to get him up must have been like moving a derrick."

"Like trying to wake the dead," Billy said. He didn't wince the way some people did now when they said "dead" or "death" in front of me.

170

"Anyway! Getting back to the point, Miss Silver, sooner or later, you're going to have to bite the bullet and transfer. You know that. You know we're not in that school district. They're letting you finish out the year. Dispensation. But the time is coming when—" He drew his hand across his throat.

I peeled the orange, thinking, *Grant . . . Patty . . . Asa . . . Jennifer. . . .* Thinking about not seeing them every day. Thinking about how I depended on seeing them. They were my friends, and more than friends. Billy used to be my friend, too, someone I could joke with, trust, depend on, someone who would even defend me from Cynthia and Mom when they were mad at me. But those were the old days. Everything was different now. Billy was different, and so was I.

"What the devil are you doing?" he said.

I looked up. "Doing? Nothing."

"You're eating the peel, for God's sake."

"No, I'm not. The white stuff inside the peel. It's good for you. Vitamins." I liked how chewy and stringy it was between my teeth. I didn't say it. It would be just another strange thing about me.

"If you're going to eat an orange, eat it like an ordinary human being," he said. "Don't go chewing on the peel. It looks pretty bad, you sitting there with that orange peel stuck in your mouth."

"Salute him, Sarabeth," Cynthia said. "Salute Sergeant Billy. He'll feel much better, won't you, Sergeant?"

"Well, what the hell," Billy said, putting his hands behind his head. "Just trying to do my best by our boarder."

Cynthia rapped his cheek with her knuckles. "Told you, she's not a boarder. Sarabeth's part of the family now, okay?"

Billy tipped back on his chair, balancing on the back legs. Behind him was the drying rack, loaded with Darren's little outfits. Shirts, undershirts, diapers, running pants. "So what do you say, member of the family?"

"I don't want to transfer, Billy. Please . . ."

I was begging, and I hated it. Hated the stinging tears behind my eyes. I forced a smile. My lips lifted. I sat up straight. No tears. No crying in front of other people. That had always been one of Mom's rules, and now it was my rule, and I wasn't going to break it.

"Well, my friend," Billy said, removing the toothpick from his mouth, "if you don't transfer, how are you going to get to school every morning? I'm telling you right now, Cynthia isn't driving you anymore. That's kaput. Finished. So it's either the bus or you got a nice thirteen- fifteen-mile distance there to cover. You going to walk? Fifteen miles, that's about four hours. So tell me, how are you going to get to school?"

"The bus," I said.

"Every day?"

"Yes."

"You have to get up at five o'clock to make it, am I right?"

"Yes."

"And you'll do that? You'll do it every morning?"

"Yes."

Billy shrugged and let the chair back down. "If you can do it, no argument from me. But no missing school. No excuses. No oversleeping. No 'I'm not feeling good enough today to get up.'"

I nodded.

"Sarabeth," Cynthia said, "are you sure? It's going to be hard. It would be a lot easier on you to transfer——"

"No," I said.

"Some mornings, you're going to be tired, and you're going to want to sleep. What then?"

"I'll get up. I'll get up every morning." I swallowed a segment of orange. It was soft and sour. "Thank you," I said to Billy. "Thank you for not——"

"Hon," Cynthia said, "you don't have to thank him."

Oh, but I did. That was another of Mom's rules: You're polite; you're always polite and careful with people who have power over your life.

21

I was never late to school now that I took a city bus; in fact, I always arrived way before first bell with time to kill. Sometimes I trotted around the track; sometimes I sat in the bleachers and read. The mornings James showed up were the best. Maybe I looked sort of excited on those days, or maybe Jen was intuitive; whichever, she picked up on our friendship, and she was so curious. She kept me asking me questions; she really wanted to know just how close James and I were. We kept having variations on the same conversation.

Jen: "I like James."

Sarabeth: "Me, too."

Jen: "He's a good friend?"

Sarabeth: "Mmm."

Jen: "How good?"

Sarabeth: "Good."

Jen: "Really good?"

Sarabeth: "Mmm."

Jen: "Really, *really* good?"

Sarabeth: "Mmm-hmm."

Partly I held back to tease her; partly I just wasn't ready to talk about James yet. Maybe I was afraid that if I said too much, I'd spoil things between us. Or maybe I was afraid that he was a fluke, a quirk, an accident, and that at any moment he would disappear as so many other things had in my life.

When I got on the bus one Friday afternoon to go to Travisino's, the first person I saw was James, sitting with his clarinet case. "Where are you going?" I said, taking the seat next to him. "I'm on this bus a lot. I've never seen you on it before."

"My music teacher changed our schedule from Saturdays to Fridays. He's in the Fischer Building downtown. Where are you going?"

"Is the Fischer Building that one on Canal Boulevard?" I asked. I didn't want to say Travisino's name and then have to explain about him. James knew some things about me, maybe even a lot, but not everything. "Is it that big brick building with all the windows?"

"Right. It used to be a shirt factory. Now it's

all music and dance studios."

"Cool," I said.

"Yeah, it's great. It's inspiring to hear all these people banging away on their instruments and blowing their lungs out."

"You make it sound like work."

"I take it you never played an instrument, Sarabeth, or you'd know it is work."

"My mom couldn't afford lessons, or an instrument," I said.

He stared at me. "Huh!"

"Huh, *what?* Huh, we were poor?"

"Hey!" He put up his hands. "Don't be sensitive."

We had sort of talked about our differences—the thing of me and Mom being trailer people and he and his family being way up there. And the thing of his being black and my being white. Which had made me ask something I really wondered about. "Does your family know about me? Would they hate me being your friend?"

"What about your family and me?"

"What family? If you could have known my

mother, you wouldn't even ask that question."

"If you were me, you'd know that I have to ask that question."

"If I were you—jeeze, oh man," I said, like Leo. Which made James laugh and say that was the corniest, most retro expression he'd heard in a long time.

We talked all the way downtown. I told him how I thought the army had ruined Billy's character. Then he got onto how he hated organized sports, and he really ranted on. I stood up to pull the cord for my stop. "James," I said, bending toward him, "you know what I think—you like to talk the way some people like to eat—nonstop."

"You saying I'm piggy?" He smiled up at me, and I thought of the first day we'd met—the bleachers, the snow, and how I'd called out, almost in a panic, when he was going to leave, and how he came back, and how that was the beginning. And remembering that, for the first time in a long time I felt lucky.

22

"Leo should be here any moment," I said to Patty as we walked out of school. "He's picking me up, and I'm hoping he's bringing Tobias, like the last time he came for me."

"You mean *the* Leo is coming here, aka Leo the Good?"

Ever since I'd told Patty that Leo had nearly cried in the storage trailer, she had looked on him as half a saint. It really annoyed me. "Right," I said. "He's driving me over to Roadview."

"How come Leo? Don't tell me you asked Cynthia and she turned you down." Patty's pale cheeks flushed. "That's going to make me really mad."

"I didn't even ask her, Patty. I just went straight to Leo."

Since the argument, or whatever it had been, over my transferring schools, I'd been careful not to ask Cynthia for any favors. I lived there, and we got along, but it was different now from when

179

I first came. It was as if a loaded paintbrush had swept across all of us and left us each stiffened and separate.

"Why are you going over to Roadview?" she said. "I thought you were through with everything there."

"I just want to see where Mom and I lived one more time. I guess it doesn't make any sense, but—"

"I can see that," Patty said. "I just hope you won't run into that Dolly woman."

Leo's truck, with the chimney sweep logo on the side, pulled up to the curb. I raised my hand to wave and, as if I'd pressed a switch, Pepper's head popped out of the window on the passenger side.

"Shoot!"

"What?" Patty said.

"That's Pepper giving me the big grin. I didn't know she was coming."

"Get over it, Sarabeth," Patty said. "Those two have been together for months. It'll be a year this summer, right?"

"Right." I looked up at the sky. Murky blue, with clouds scooting east to west. It was warm today. We were in the middle of a late-January thaw.

"And it looks as if it's going to stick," Patty went on.

"Maybe."

"Oh, come on. Same thing with, I hate to say it, my mother and whatsisbadface, the stepfather."

I took Mom's fish scarf from my backpack and tied it through a loop on my jeans. "Have you gotten over it with whatsisbadface, the step-father, Patty?"

"No," she admitted.

"So, I'm that way with Pepper. I haven't gotten over it, and I never will. You can't believe how she acts, as if she loves and adores me to the sky."

"Maybe she does. Give her a break."

We went down the steps together. "You always think the best of everyone's motives," I said.

"Please. How can you say that when you know how nasty I feel about my stepfather? But I really think you could give up being so mad at Pepper. What has she done to you? Not her fault about your mother, and she takes care of Tobias. Doesn't she get some credit for that?"

"You're right, Patty, I know you're right. I

should like her. She's probably a very okay person, who I'm not giving a chance because *I'm* not a very okay person! The truth is, I can hardly stand being near her!"

"Shh!" Patty took me by the arm, moved me closer to her. "Don't do that to yourself. Don't go there. Will you be okay?"

"I won't fall apart, if that's what you mean."

She squeezed my arm. "I'll see you tomorrow. And you *are* an okay person. Please remember that."

"Tomorrow," I said, and I walked toward the truck.

Pepper called out my name and gave me a big, big smile.

"Hey, Leo," I said.

"Hey, Sarabeth. Ready?" He leaned past Pepper to look at me, and I met his eyes, the way I hadn't met hers. "Are you sure you want to do this?" he asked. "Because it's okay with me if you change your mind."

"Leo, I'm not changing my mind."

I scrambled into the passenger seat next to Pepper. She was wearing some kind of spicy perfume that knifed straight into my temples.

"Just give me a little push if you need more room," she said as Leo pulled out into traffic. "So you phoned the people who live there now, Sarabeth, and they know you're coming?"

I hadn't thought for a moment about phoning. I'd just imagined myself being there, where Mom and I had lived. Dumb.

"Sarabeth, Pepper and I were talking about this," Leo said, glancing over at me. "Talking about what you're doing by going over there, and Pepper was saying that this is really something you have to do." He sat on the horn for a moment as a black car cut him off at the corner.

"A necessary part of the grief process," Pepper said.

"Pepper says if you want to do this, you need to do it."

I sat still, fingering my fish scarf. I couldn't remember Leo's ever quoting Mom like that, as if she had the wisdom of the ages.

"Pepper says when you leave a place where you lived all your life—"

"I didn't live there all my life, Leo."

"Hey, you did. What're you talking about?"

"We lived in Two for two years. Before, we

lived over in Sixteen. You know that!"

Leo stopped at the red light under the bridge, just before the turn for the highway. "What I meant was that Roadview was where you lived all your life. Pepper got it right on that, didn't she? She said—"

"Leo, stop with the 'Pepper says' stuff," Pepper interrupted. "I'm starting to feel like a parrot! I can talk for myself."

"Yeah, Leo," I said.

"Jeeze, oh man, you two, don't go ganging up on me."

"We will if we want to," Pepper sang out. She put up her hand to me for a confirming slap, and then, as if I didn't know what that up-stretched palm meant, she said, "Gimme five!"

I resisted the urge to tell her she was way out-of-date. Way uncool. I held up my palm, and she slapped it, smiling as if this proved we were friends.

"Tell Sarabeth what you said about her saying good-bye to the place, Pep," Leo said.

Pep. What a dumb nickname. I inched closer to the window.

"The way I see it, Sarabeth," Pepper said, breathing in my ear, "you left your home too fast. No warning. No chance to say good-bye. One day you're there and, then, sad to say, the next day you're not. And besides everything else you went through, that alone is just so disorienting, so traumatizing."

I focused on her backpack. Leather, like her jacket. Not very practical. Leather was heavy and expensive. She could afford it, though; she taught at community college, probably made oodles of money.

"Everyone needs to say good-bye to the things they love and have to leave," she was saying. "We invest emotionally in our things, as well as in people. A lot of folks don't like to admit that; maybe they're a little ashamed of it. Too materialistic."

"Mmm . . . mmmm," I said, and thought how funny it was—or not so funny—that Leo had gone from Mom, who cleaned houses and never had a spare dime, to Pepper, who was a professor and bought herself silver bracelets and leather jackets.

"People make the mistake of thinking that they don't need to say good-bye to the chairs they sat in and the beds they slept in and the house that held those things. Now, you, Sarabeth, you're not making that mistake. This is wise of you, really! What you're doing today, very good. I applaud you."

"Smart cookie, this Pepper," Leo said. "Right, Sarabeth?"

I didn't answer, just stared ahead. Let Leo say what he wanted to about Pepper; I didn't have to agree.

Now he was driving with his left hand, and his right arm had snaked across the back of the seat, his hand moving for my head. I leaned away, toward the window, remembering something that happened in our kitchen a year ago, or maybe it was two years ago. Mom and I and Leo had been sitting around, talking or eating. I didn't remember that part, just how, suddenly, I'd gone for Leo's head and messed up his hair good. No reason. I'd just felt like doing it, to be funny or cute, or maybe, really, because I loved him. I had loved him a lot back then, but not now. No more.

Now he was talking about his work, how this

was the busy season, how people all of a sudden remembered they should have had their chimneys cleaned months ago, before the cold weather set in, and how his phone never stopped ringing off the hook.

I had heard it all before. Every year, Leo went through the same routine. I even knew what he'd say next, and he said it.

"Everyone wants their chimneys done PDQ. You should see the messages on the machine."

"What's PDQ?" Pepper asked, sitting up very straight, like the smartest girl in the classroom, or the teacher's pet.

"Professor Pepper," Leo said. "You amaze me. Everyone knows PDQ."

"Well, I don't," Pepper said.

"Oh, I can't believe this. Sarabeth knows. Sarabeth, tell Pepper pretty damn quick, before she has a fit, pretty damn quick, what PDQ means. Wink wink."

"Oh, duuuh. I should have guessed," Pepper said.

Leo turned up the hill that led to Roadview. The wet road squeaked under the tires. He pulled up in front of our house and cut the engine. It looked the same, except that a yellow bike with a blue stripe down the fender lay in the yard.

"Well . . . here we are," Leo said. "Sarabeth . . . are you sure now that you want to do this?"

I slid out of the truck and walked toward the kitchen door. There was a light on in the kitchen, another in the living room. I knocked and, after a moment, the door opened with the same creaky noise it had always made. A woman, wearing slacks and a white shirt, looked out at me. "If you're selling magazines, sorry, but forget it."

"I'm not selling anything," I said. "I used to live here. I was wondering, could I come in and just look around?"

"You were the people before us? What's your name?"

"Silver. Sarabeth Silver."

She stared past me to Leo's truck. "Who's that, your parents? What kind of truck is that?"

"They're my friends. Leo's a chimney sweep. That's a picture of a sweep on the side, with the top hat and—"

"Your mother know you're here with him?"

"Yes."

She twisted her mouth to one side and waited,

as if she hoped I would go away. Then she shrugged and opened the door wide enough for me to follow her inside. Right away, I saw that the kitchen floor had been recovered, our old wheezy fridge replaced, and the walls repainted. "It looks nice," I said.

"We fixed it up," she said. "Went through the place with a fine-tooth comb."

My ears flamed. A fine-tooth comb was what you used to get rid of cootie eggs. I followed her into the living room. Couch, rug, lamps, everything new-looking, clean, perfect. Stuffed animals crowded the windowsill. "My hobby," she said, straightening a tiger's ear. "Mama's toys. You want to see the bedrooms now?"

From the doorway of what had been my room, I saw a double-decker bed, hockey posters, matching curtains and bedspreads, hockey sticks leaning against the wall. In a daze, I went to Mom's room. Another blur of furniture and curtains. I looked and stepped back. At night, when I hadn't been able to sleep, I would think of these rooms, walk through them, look at our familiar things, touch them, smell them: our clothes in the closets, the flowered plates in the cupboard, every one different, and the Princess Di photo that Mom had framed and hung on her bedroom wall. In my mind, I would curl up on the velvet couch or lie on my bed or pull a chair up to the kitchen table to look again at the scratches and burns I knew by heart.

But now I was here, and nothing was the way I remembered it. Not one thing in these rooms, not a scrap, showed that our life together, the history of us, had even existed.

Had there even been an *us*? How could I be sure that we *had* lived here? Where was the proof? How did I know that what I remembered was true?

23

"She's upset," Leo said, watching me as I climbed back into the truck. "She doesn't have to say a word—I can see it. . . . Sarabeth, I'm taking you for an ice cream before we do anything else."

"Good idea," Pepper said.

"I don't want ice cream," I said.

"How about a soda?" Leo turned the key in the ignition. "You need a little sugar rush. I bet your adrenaline is down to zip. Does a soda sound good? Ice cream soda, or regular soda?"

"Neither, Leo."

All through the years when Leo was Mom's friend, he would come over on the weekends with a bag of groceries and make a meal for us. Half the stuff he brought had names that we'd never even heard: hummus, babaganoush, gomasao. He loved food, loved to buy it, loved to cook it. Mom said that Leo thought food was at least half the solution to every problem.

"Come on, Sarabeth, let me get you something," he coaxed. "You want a sandwich? We can tool right over to Basario's and—"

"Leo, I said no. Be quiet about food!"

"You know what, Sarabeth?" He turned off the key with a sharp click. "You're just like your mom sometimes, hardheaded and stubborn as hell."

"Good! Thank you!" I reached for my back-pack and held it against my stomach, held it there, solid, the books pressing into me through my jacket.

Into the silence that fell then, Pepper said in a conciliatory tone, "Look at the sky, you two. Look what's happening to the weather."

The wisps of clouds had knitted together and become a gray quilt completely covering the blue.

"So, we had our bit of warm weather," Leo said finally. "Now it's going to snow to remind us it's still winter."

"Leo, do you remember us living there?" I pointed to our trailer.

"You and Jane?" He started the motor again. "Jeeze, oh man, what kind of question is that?"

"A question, Leo, just a question!" I wanted to hear him say, Yes, I remember you and Jane living there. Yes, your life together was real.

The truck eased forward. "Funny question, Sarabeth."

I sat on the edge of the seat, wondering how I could ever have liked this truck with its ashy smell and cold fake leather seats. "Leo, do you remember us or not?"

"You're in such a weird mood today, Sarabeth. Isn't the answer pretty obvious?"

"Say it, Leo! Yes or no?"

"Yes! Of course. What do you think?" Leaning on the steering wheel, Leo rolled the truck slowly through the trailer park. "I'm never going to forget Jane."

"Maybe you did already," I said. "If you'd married Mom, instead of dumping her, maybe everything would be different right now."

"What?" His hand hit the horn and flew off. "I guess you forgot, Sarabeth. Your mother was the one who kept pushing me off; she was the one who broke us up, saying I was too young, or whatever dumb reasons she had."

"Don't you call her dumb," I shouted. We were rolling down the hill now, the same hill Mom and I had run down, hand in hand. "Don't dare talk about Mom like that, and here's something else. Don't ever talk to me again, Leo, not ever again!"

"You're out of your mind, Sarabeth," he shouted back.

"Stop," Pepper said, turning from one of us to the other. "Stop that, you two."

"You know what, Sarabeth," Leo said, looking at me, letting the truck drive itself, "you've been weird ever since your mother died; even Cynthia says so. She says you're just not the same person."

The truck sped forward. The highway was in front of us, like the cross on a T.

"Leo, watch it!" Pepper cried.

He jerked the wheel to the right, and the truck turned with a screech and a hard, jouncing jolt. Then we were off the road, tipped nose-first into the ditch. A car passed, then another. A horn tooted. "Oh my God," Pepper breathed.

I straightened up, uncrinking my neck. It was my fault Leo had gone off the road. I'd said something, I couldn't remember what, but something to unnerve him. I wiped my sweaty hands on the fish scarf. Never upset the driver. Was that another one of Mom's "Rules for Life"? If it wasn't, it should have been.

Now we should all get out and push the truck out of the ditch. I'd pushed with Mom plenty of times when our battery died, or we ran out of gas or had some other minor catastrophe.

Mom would put the car in neutral, and then we'd both get out, Mom on the driver's side, with her hand through the window to steer, me on the passenger side. "Heave ho!" Mom would say, and, then, one, two, three, we'd push and get the car moving again. That's what we had to do now. Heave ho. One, two, three, and we'd have the truck out of the ditch and onto the road.

All this went through my mind in a split second.

In the next moment, I seemed to be outside the truck and looking in. Observing the people there. Observing Sarabeth, long-haired girl tipped forward, spine like a lightning rod. And Leo, swiveled toward her, big head emerging from his jacket like a startled turtle. Sitting between them, pulling at her fingers, Pepper.

"Sarabeth," Leo said. "Are you okay? Sarabeth?

Hey! Give me an answer." He reached across Pepper and slapped my face.

Then I was back inside the truck, the seat cold under me, my cheek stinging. Leo had slapped me! I wrenched open the door and fell out of the truck. I scrambled to my feet, climbed out of the ditch, and walked away, down the road.

Behind me, Leo tapped the horn and yelled out the window. "Sarabeth, come back here. Come back here!"

"Go to hell, Leo," I said. Why did he slap me? What right did he have? Then Pepper was behind me, calling for me to wait for her. I kept walking.

"Sarabeth." She caught up to me. "Leo's crying," she said, trying to take my arm. "He thinks he hurt you. First, the truck in the ditch and then—"

I walked faster.

"He didn't mean it like a real slap," she said, hurrying to keep up with me. "He was sort of overcome, and he got scared. You looked so spacey. I was scared, too! Sarabeth, you know Leo—he's got the heart of a girl; he would never deliberately hurt you."

"Stop talking to me about Leo," I said.

"No, I won't! You have to listen to me." She grabbed my arm and held it, slowing me down. "He loves you; you know he does. Look at him, Sarabeth. He's *crying!*"

She swiveled me around to face the truck. I pushed her off, but she grabbed me again, surprising me with her strength. She must lift weights, I thought.

"Look!" she said. Her narrow, pointed face was drawn up into a fierce, doglike scowl. "Look at him, Sarabeth!"

But all I could see was the truck in the ditch and the top of Leo's head bent over the steering wheel. Was he crying? Maybe. "Tell him I'm okay," I said.

"No, you tell him. Go back and tell him. He feels awful; you can't leave him like that. My God! Have a heart!"

I walked slowly back to the truck and stood by the window. Leo lifted his head, and I wanted to slap his face, slap away that sad look. Pepper was walking back toward us. I imagined her seeing me slap Leo. Why didn't I do it, instead of just thinking about it? Why did I always think about things, never do them?

"You don't really believe I forgot Jane, do you?" Leo said. He looked at me with red, wet eyes.

Patty was right. He was good. I was the one who was messed up. I stood there, thinking this, and then I reached through the window and touched his hand. "I know you didn't forget Mom, Leo," I said. "I know that."

24

February was usually the worst month of the winter, but we were halfway through it, and the temperature had been staying up in the twenties. That made it easier to put in my time on the bleachers before the bell rang. A lot more comfortable to talk to James, too. Wednesday morning, we walked around the track, in step, so concentrated on our conversation that we almost missed hearing the bell.

"I have no experience of death," James said. "All my grandparents are still living, and my cousins, the whole family. I guess I'm just lucky." He held my arm for a moment. "Is it okay with you that I said that?"

I nodded.

"My father wants me to go to Harvard when I graduate," James said. "He wants me to do what he didn't do. I know that Harvard could be great, but I'm thinking I should go to a historically black college, one of those schools that have been around doing their job for us when we couldn't get into Harvard or Brown, or anywhere else. I'm thinking, I should support them; it's the right thing to do."

"I admire people with principles," I said.

"How about you? Where are you thinking of going?"

"I don't know. It's a money thing; plus, I don't know where I could get in. My grades . . ."

I'd been near the top of my class when Mom was around to goad me, and I used to like school, but I'd lost interest. I didn't keep up with my work. I had let things slide.

"What about community college?" James said. "No, forget I said that. You can aim higher. What do you want to do?"

I started to say that I didn't have a clue, but this was James. I didn't want him thinking I was a dope. So, as if it was a real thought, I said, "Premed."

"Excellent. Same here. I'll be a physician, though I might change my mind and go for physics. Maybe I'll do double degrees. They can work together."

He started talking about an article he'd read about dark energy. Whatever that is, I thought.

Maybe it was what I had—dark energy draining me of the will to do any of the things I used to do.

"And so they're saying, theorizing, really, that the dark energy of the universe weighs more than all visible matter and dark matter together. It's amazing."

I nodded. When we were on everyday stuff, I could keep up with him, but when he got going on black holes, exploding stars, protons, and neutrons, I just sort of staggered along behind him, doing my best to follow him into the quarks and wimps world. Or maybe I should say the quarks and wimps universe or megaverse, which was a word I'd learned from James, of course.

"Maybe all the dead souls are actually what make the dark energy of the universe," I said.

"Nice try," he said. He had such a smile! "But dark energy was here billions of years before humans."

That was when the bell rang. We walked across the field toward the building. "James, you're going to be famous someday," I said. "That's my prediction, and then you won't even talk to me anymore."

"I'll always talk to you."

"Even when you get the Nobel Prize?"

"Even then. I won't forget the little people in my life."

"Oh, thank you, I'm grateful already."

We went up the steps and through the door. "See you later," he said. The back of his hand grazed my cheek. He bounded away, and I watched him go, wishing he'd come back, wanting to feel his hand on my cheek again and be in the warmth of his smile.

25

"Kiddo, pay attention, and you'll learn something," Billy said.

Saturday morning and, miracle of miracles, I was standing at Billy's elbow, by invitation, watching him mix pancake batter in a yellow bowl.

"Did your mom teach you how to make pancakes from scratch?" he asked.

"No, we always had the stuff from a box."

Billy made a disapproving sound with his tongue. "It's part of your basic culinary education."

I pushed up the sleeves of my sweatshirt. "Lots of Sundays, Mom had to work. She didn't have time for stuff like this."

Outside, it was raining, the sixth day of straight rain, but inside, it was hot. The radiators were clanging, and heat was pouring into the apartment. Billy was wearing boxers and sneakers, and I was thinking about changing into cutoffs and a sleeveless top.

"These pancakes are going to be the best you

ever had, way superior to what comes out of a box." He broke another egg, dropping the yolk into one bowl, the white into another. "Remember, you gotta whip the egg whites separately."

I tried to look really interested, so he'd know that I appreciated his doing this with me. I'd been reading, actually rereading *Jane Eyre*, a book Mrs. Hilbert had given me, when Billy called to ask if I wanted to learn to make pancakes the "right" way.

Not really had been my instant reaction, but then I thought better of it and put down my book. Now I was glad that I had. This was the best time I'd had with Billy since I'd moved in. Also, it was kind of nostalgic for me. I used to really love cooking. I thought I wanted to be a chef, and I'd even picked out the place where I'd study, the New England Culinary Institute in Vermont.

Billy sprinkled cinnamon into the dry mix. "Not too much, not too little."

"Right."

He turned on the heat under the pan. "You want the pan good and hot, but you have to watch it. Not so hot the pancakes come out hard."

"Right."

"Billy, look at you," Cynthia said, coming into the kitchen. She was holding Darren under one arm in the sack of potatoes position.

"Look at me, what? Hey, big guy," he said, tipping his head over to speak to Darren.

"You're in your boxers, and—"

Billy poured a spoonful of batter onto the pan. It hissed, and bubbles popped. "Perfect! You see that, Sarabeth?"

"—Sarabeth is right here," Cynthia finished.

"Yes, she is," Billy agreed. "Learning the secrets of the master chef. You up for pancakes?"

Darren bounced in his mother's arms and yelled something that sounded vaguely like "I sure am!"

"Sarabeth isn't a little girl anymore." Cynthia put Darren into his chair and locked in the tray. "She's a teenager. You don't go half-dressed in your underwear around a teenage girl."

"Afraid she's gonna get aroused by my hairy legs?" He poured another spoonful of batter onto the pan.

"I don't mind his boxers, Cynthia," I said.

"Keep out of this, Sarabeth; this is between me and Billy."

"Aw, Cynthia, give it a rest," Billy said. "These are shorts I'm wearing. I could go outside this way. That's all these are, shorts."

"Underwear," Cynthia said. She sat down and started feeding Darren from a little jar of apple-sauce.

"I'm not going to be corrupted," I said. I got a glass of juice and sat on the high stool in the corner.

"I told you, be quiet, Sarabeth." She gave me the tag end of the glare she'd fixed on Billy. "Billy, just go put on some clothes, okay?"

"No. I'm not going to do that."

"Don't fight me on this."

"Damn, Cynthia! I do my job all week and then I come home for the weekend, and right away you're after me, saying I'm not trying with her." He pointed the spatula at me. "Telling me I ought to be more like a father, be friendlier, do something with her, so okay, I'm doing it! I'm teaching her to make pancakes, and then you come in, and now it's I'm wearing boxers—"

"Billy—" Cynthia said.

"Well, big deal! This is my home. Or it was. I thought it was. Not very big, not much room, and a lot less room since we got ourselves a boarder. Well, okay, that's the way it is, but at least I'm going to be comfortable when I'm here. And I'm comfortable this way. I'm not changing into pants and a belt and a tie. And that's my last word on this nonsense."

"I didn't say a tie," Cynthia said. "And don't give me that 'last word' stuff. If we're having an argument, let's have it."

"You might as well have said tie." Now he was pointing the spatula at Cynthia. "You're just about strangling me with all your ideas about everything. You want to strangle me, don't you?"

"Yeah, Billy, I do," she said. "I could do it, right now, with extreme pleasure."

"Well, go ahead! Just try. Here!" He grabbed a dish towel and threw it at her. "Maybe that'll work. Here!" He threw another dish towel. Then he grabbed the frying pan by the handle and banged it on the stove hard and loud.

Darren was wailing. Cynthia scooped him out of his chair and held him close to her chest. "Billy," she cried. "What are you doing? I'm just asking you to wear some clothes; I'm not asking you to leap off a cliff."

"If I want to wear my damn boxers in my own damn kitchen, I'm going to damn well do it!"

"What's wrong with you? Stop it! You're scaring the baby."

"There's nothing wrong with me that some space and privacy won't fix," Billy yelled, and now *he* was glaring, but not at Cynthia. At me. "Get her out of here! Give her to someone else. Give me back my home. Let her be someone else's problem."

"Billy!" Cynthia said again.

I slid off the stool and went into the other room, out the door, into the hall, and down the stairs.

Outside, the rain was coming down steadily, and the wind blew hard, picking up papers and flattening them against the buildings. I turned left, in the opposite direction from the way that I went every morning to get the bus. I didn't know where I was going. I wasn't going anywhere. I was just going. I was wet in a moment, and I hunched over, as if I could protect myself from the weather.

26

Darren was standing in his crib, shaking the bars. "Sarabeee!" he greeted me.

"Hello, baby."

It was as warm and dry today as yesterday had been cold and wet. The noon sun slanted in through the bedroom window, laying a square of harsh color on the floor.

March: lion and lamb, like Billy. Yesterday morning, he had started as the lamb and turned into the lion. Since then, we had hardly spoken. I had stayed in bed this morning until he went out for the newspaper. While he ate his breakfast, I read, trying to get lost in the story and forget his waving the spatula and yelling, "Get her out of here! Give her to someone else."

All through the night, those words had been in my head. I hadn't slept a lot. My mind raced, thinking how Billy and Cynthia had had their life all set, their little apartment, their baby, their work, and then they got stuck with me. And no matter what Cynthia said about their loving me to pieces, it was the pieces part I felt most, not the love part.

I kept looking for a plan, seeking a way out of the trap I was in.

"Sarabeee!" Darren screamed. His face was red and sweaty. "Out! Out! Me walk!" He shook the bars as if he was in a cage. If I climbed in with him, we could both shake the bars, two prisoners together.

I reached in and lifted him out of the crib. "Yeah! Good!" he cried, patting my face with his heavy little paw.

Cynthia and Billy had gone for a ride. Maybe they would talk about me and make their own plan. Cynthia had asked me to baby-sit Darren, and when they left, she gave me a significant look, as if to say, See, I trust you.

I changed Darren and carried him down the stairs. When we were outside, I turned right and walked toward the corner of Court Boulevard, as if I had a destination. As if the Plan was in place. Darren was big for his age, heavy and active. He wriggled and jumped in my arms, didn't hold still for a moment. He drooled on my face and pulled my hair. "He's a pistol," Cynthia said

211

whenever she talked about him.

I walked briskly for about twenty minutes; then my arms began to ache, and I slowed down. "Sassabeee," Darren snorted in my ear.

"Yeah, do you think you could take it easy?" I kept shifting his weight. "Give me a break, will you?"

"Walk!" he said in my ear. "Down! Walk!"

"Okay. Good idea."

Now we walked, holding hands. He was pretty steady on his feet, but slow and meandering. He didn't know what a straight line meant. He was like a dog: He had to stop and investigate every crack in the sidewalk, every fire hydrant, every scrap of filthy paper on the pavement.

The breeze was cool on my face. I didn't know where I was going, but I was moving. That was what counted. That made sense. It was important. I was going somewhere. Somewhere else. Someplace that wasn't the apartment. Someplace with no Billy.

That last thought transfixed me. All my weariness dropped away. My mind was extraordinarily clear. The Plan snapped into place, and it was very simple and very easy. I was going away with Darren. That was the Plan. Just the two of us. We would go away together and make a little family of our own. How? Easy. I'd get on a bus and let my instincts guide me. My instincts would tell me when to stop. "Do it your own way," that woman had said to me weeks ago, and now I knew that this was what she had meant.

This was my own way. Wherever I stopped would be a good place, and Darren and I would be happy together. I'd take care of him, good care, the best care. Lately, Cynthia had been letting me do more for him, and I knew how to do everything he needed, how to change his diapers, make his food, sing him to sleep.

We'd stay together, never leave each other. It would be Darren, me, and Tobias. Tobias! I couldn't leave him behind. I'd have to go to Leo's place and get him. I hurried, holding Darren's hand. I turned a corner. I was on a street of stores. I picked Darren up and walked faster. People were out in clusters, and they parted for me. It was a beautiful day, the sun, the little breeze, the puffy clouds. Everything was good. I had a plan. I kept telling myself I had a plan.

"Oooh, a baby," a woman said, smiling at us.

Did she think Darren was my baby? That was a good sign. An omen!

A girl wearing jeans and high heels was sitting on the sidewalk, her back against a building, holding a handwritten sign: LADY DOWN ON HER LUCK. Another omen! That was me, Girl Down on Her Luck. The girl was beautiful, with long blond hair. A prom queen–type girl. She had a paper cup for money next to her. If I'd had dollar bills, I would have given them all to her, but I didn't want to insult her with change.

I hurried past. Darren chewed on his fist and giggled in my ear. He patted my face and made goofy sounds. His face was fat and cute. A few drops of rain fell. "Raining, wet," he said. He looked pleased with himself.

"Sun shower," I said. That was good. I was teaching him.

Two women approached, both smoking cigars and wearing tiger-striped coats. Their coats bothered me. I walked purposefully, clutching Darren. I was doing something, going somewhere. I had the Plan. I turned another corner. A man was ahead of me, wearing a black overcoat, talking on

214

a cell phone. I passed him, then another man on a cell phone, also wearing a black overcoat. Maybe they were twins. Or maybe the same man.

Maybe I was dreaming all this. That would explain so much! It would explain why everything was so bizarre. Women smoking cigars. Prom queens begging. Even my carrying Darren was bizarre. He was so heavy. I heaved him up again.

A thin-faced man with wild hair put out his hand to me. "Hello! You look like a kind person. Can I ask you something without seeming rude?" He spoke fast, urgently. "I'm not a drug addict; I'm a stage designer, I'm locked out of my apartment. All my stuff is on the street. I'm locked out of my life. Can you give me a quarter to call my mother?"

I gave him a quarter, but he followed me down the street. "Can you give me another quarter, kind person? Just a quarter. I need a cup of coffee. That's a cute baby. A quarter, that's all."

I walked faster. Horns blared. A screech of tires. I was in the middle of a road, clutching Darren. Cars passed on both sides, their hot breath on my legs. "Get out of the road, you idiot," a man yelled. "You wanna get killed, you and the kid?"

I plunged forward. I was on the sidewalk again. I held Darren tightly, shaking. I was crying, but without tears, just sounds.

I found my way back to the apartment. It wasn't that far. I had gone in a wide circle. I changed Darren's diaper, washed his face, and gave him a bottle of juice. I put him in his crib and sang him a song. Then I washed my own hands and face, drank three glasses of water, and lay down on the couch.

I slept without waking for ten hours. When I woke up, I was sane again. But I still needed a plan, only this time, a real one.

27

"Sarabeth," Patty said into the dark, "are you sleeping?"

"I'm awake, Patty." I turned to lie on my side, facing her bed. Our beds were separated by a night table. It was near midnight, her house was quiet, and outside, the street was quiet, too, much quieter than where Cynthia and Billy lived.

"Did you hear me talking to you?" she said.

"No."

"Maybe you were sleeping."

"I said I wasn't!" Anger flashed through me. A zing of heat in my stomach. Senseless anger. Pointless. It came at me like that now, and I was never prepared for it.

"I asked you a question and you didn't answer," Patty said. "I was sure you were sleeping."

"Maybe I . . . zoned out." I kept my voice neutral, flat. The heat in my belly flattened out, too.

"Where did you go?" She gave a little laugh. "What zone were you in?"

"I was just drifting. Thinking, I guess."

"About what?"

"Nothing, really." Just the usual stuff stomping around in my mind. Thoughts and feelings like restless, heavy boots. Thoughts about Mom, the future, where I should live, what I should do. Sometimes the boots got lighter and James thoughts sneaked in.

"You were thinking about something," Patty said. "You can tell me." She leaned over the divide between the beds and caught at my arm. "Sarabeth . . . I'm worried about you. I want to help you, but you don't let me. You don't let any of us. I want to make a difference for you. You're my friend, and I love you. I want to balance out a little what you did for me."

"I didn't do anything for you, Patty."

"You did, and I haven't forgotten. You helped me when I needed help, you and your mom. She was so great——"

"Don't talk about her," I said.

"Okay, I won't! Not now, anyway. Sarabeth, I know you're proud and independent, but everyone has needs; it's nothing to be ashamed of. All of us want to help you—Jennifer, Asa, Grant—

it's not just me. All our hearts are with you and we're all worried about you. You know what Grant said the other day? I thought it was wise. She said everything has a meaning, but you just might not know it now. She said if you could only believe that, it might help you."

"I'm fine," I said.

"Sarabeth, are you listening to me? Did you hear what I said? Do you even hear yourself?"

"Yes, sure."

"No. You don't hear yourself. You don't hear anyone anymore. You don't let anyone in anymore. You're all closed up; you're like a room with no doors and no windows. Please let me in. Please let me help you."

I knew her outburst was from the heart, and it touched me. I wasn't cold and unfeeling. I wasn't heartless and numb. Not completely. Not yet. I heard her words; I didn't close them out.

But yet, I didn't answer. I let silence grow between us. I didn't speak. I lay there and said nothing.

And Patty, still leaning over from her bed, her hand still on my arm, waited. I could hear her breathing, I could hear her waiting. Waiting for me to speak, to break myself open, to show her there was a window in me and that she wasn't closed out.

I knew this was what she wanted and, in a way, I wanted to give it to her. But I didn't do it. My thoughts wandered. I let my mind drift away, and when I broke the silence, it was to speak about something else.

"Patty, do you know that this is the first time I've lived in a house with stairs? And two bathrooms? And a room just for eating and another just for TV?"

"Well, what can I say?" Patty fell back on her own bed. "I'm glad for you."

I knew what I'd done. My throat tightened. Why couldn't I make anyone happy anymore? I sat up, folding my arms around my knees. "I've been living with your family almost three weeks now. It'll be three weeks on Sunday."

"I'm glad you came to us," Patty said after a moment.

"Your stepfather isn't glad."

"Oh, him. Kevin's a jerk. You know that. A total hard case."

"He's a lawyer; he's educated. You have to respect that."

It was something Mom would have said. I was being a parrot. Maybe I did respect his education, but I didn't like him any more than Patty did.

"Every time you go for a walk," she said, "he's waiting to cross-examine you when you come back. Where were you? What did you do? Who did you see? What does he think you're doing, robbing houses? How educated is that?"

"Actually, your mom's not too happy about my being here, either," I said. "She asked me how long I planned to stay."

"Sarabeth, she didn't!" Patty turned on the light on the night table.

I blinked and covered my eyes. "Yeah, she did. So . . . it seems like I should think about going."

"When did she say that to you?"

"Tonight."

Patty threw aside her blanket. "Why did she say that? Oh, I know why! It's Kevin. He's got such an influence on her. She'll do anything he says. Ever since she married him, she thinks she's Juliet and he's Romeo. She's flipped completely! He's made her bizarre and selfish."

"I told her I'd be leaving pretty soon. I always

221

knew it was temporary, Patty. I told your mom that, I told her I was only wanting to give Cynthia and Billy a break from me."

"You're not going back there." She was out of bed now and pacing. "I won't allow it. It's perfect your being here; it's perfect for both of us. You get a home, and I get to think about someone besides Kevin. And it's working; it's working for both of us. You know what they say. If it ain't broke, don't fix it."

I smoothed the blanket over my knees. Patty was wrong. It wasn't working and it wasn't going to work. Her stepfather was too opposed to me. I thought she was right about one thing, though. From what I'd seen, her mom followed anything he said.

"I can't believe my mother said for you to go."

"She didn't really put it that way, Patty."

"But that's what she meant. I wish she was even half as nice, half as sweet as your mother was to me."

"Sweet? *Mom?* She'd laugh her head off if she heard that. She'd tell you she didn't have a sweet bone in her body."

"Sarabeth, come on! Your mother was great."
Patty sat down at the foot of my bed. "Look how
she let me live with you last year when I needed
someplace."

"Well, that was different. Your uncle was
abusing you! You had to go someplace."

"You and your mom didn't live in exactly a
palace of space. She didn't have to take me in. She
was good. She was always so okay about my being
there. I think she even liked it."

"Yeah, she did. She liked it for me. She liked
my having company. You're right," I said, my face
falling onto my knees. "She was good."

And that last night came back to me again so
vividly. Mom in her red dress, the two of us running through the rain, hand in hand. She'd been
laughing, and I kept telling her to be quiet, and
neither of us knew that with each moment that
passed, she was already dying, her heart starting
to fail her, her body getting ready to separate her
from her life, from me.

"Sarabeth?" Patty put her hand on my head.
"What are you thinking about now?"

"I'm fine," I said automatically, and I burst

into tears. I cried as I hadn't cried in weeks, in months. I couldn't stop crying.

"Sarabeth," Patty said. "Oh, Sarabeth. I know, I know . . . Poor thing. Poor baby." She stroked my head.

I pushed her hand away. "Stop pitying me."

"I don't pity you, Sarabeth. I don't! You say that all the time. 'Don't pity me.' It's not pity! Can't you tell the difference? It's sympathy. I understand. We all do. The worst has happened to you, but, Sarabeth, when is it going to end? You can't be depressed forever."

I straightened up. Mom would have been proud of my posture. "Sympathy or pity, it's the same," I said. "Awful. And I'm not depressed, Patty."

She shrugged. "If you say so." She went to the bureau and took a cigarette and a pack of matches from her purse.

"You shouldn't smoke," I said, still sitting rigidly upright. "It makes me furious when I see you smoking."

"Kevin smokes, and he's got my mother smoking, so why not me?" The cigarette was between her lips. She kept trying to light the match. She finally got it going, and smoke traveled up around her face. She narrowed her eyes; they were shaped like tiny blue diamonds.

"Smoke is going to make your skin wrinkled. You have beautiful skin," I said. "It's perfect now. Smoke will ruin it."

"So, maybe by the time I'm forty, I'll get wrinkles. I'll be dead by then anyway."

"Now you sound depressed," I said.

But maybe she was right. Mom hadn't smoked, never drank more than a single beer at a time. She was a little goofy sometimes, but she worked hard, she was honest, and what did it all mean? She died anyway, not even thirty years old. She never made it to forty, not anywhere near.

28

W hen I moved back in again with Cynthia
and Billy, I found that they had rearranged
things. For instance, the little bureau was filled
with Darren's stuff now, and Cynthia had cleared
out a kitchen cupboard for me to use. "You actually have more room this way," she said. She had
given me two shelves below the counter. "And it's
neater, isn't it?" She was right. Before, even with
the bureau, most of my stuff had been stowed in
plastic garbage bags, and every morning, getting
dressed, I had found myself thinking how ticked
off Mom would be to see me becoming the undis-
puted queen of wrinkles.

The main thing that was different now,
though, was that I didn't have a "room" anymore. Cynthia and Billy had moved the couch
out into the room and turned it to face the TV.
"Maybe we'll switch back to the way you had it,
after a while," Cynthia said. "Let's see how this
works out for now."

In the weeks I'd been away, Billy had gotten

used to having the couch available whenever he wanted it. "But it's still your place," he said to me. "You're the one who sleeps here, so you have priority." I saw Cynthia nod approvingly. "You just give me the signal, whenever you're ready to go to sleep or whatever, and I'll clear out."

Cynthia must have talked to him about how to act with me. He was nice, almost the way he used to be back in the days when they had lived near Mom and me. The first day I was back in the apartment, he seemed sort of glad to see me. He gave me a hug and made a joke about pancakes.

I wanted things to work out. I think we all did. But something had changed. We were wary around one another, sometimes too polite, sometimes too tense. I think we were all afraid of another blowup.

"I talked to your social worker this morning," Cynthia said one afternoon when I got home from school.

I unloaded my books onto the couch and went into the kitchen. Cynthia was mixing a salad in the same big yellow bowl in which Billy had mixed pancake batter. "What did he want?" I asked.

"He said—what is his name anyway? Is it Tavero?"

"Travisino."

"Oh, right, that's it, Travisino. I don't know why I can't remember that name. Anyway, he said you'd missed the last two appointments. Is that so?"

"If he says it, it must be."

"If he says it—what do you say?"

I took a piece of onion and chewed it. "Okay. Sure."

"'Okay. Sure'? What does that mean, Sarabeth?"

"Whatever, Cynthia. I'm just being agreeable."

"Sarabeth." She looked at me mournfully. "What's the matter with you? You don't seem like the same girl anymore."

I wanted to laugh. The same girl? The same as *what*? The same as I'd been when I lived with Mom? The same idiot who believed, because her mother had told her, that life was like a river and you just had to learn to swim and stay afloat? The same fool who thought everything could be fixed, every problem solved, every stumbling block overcome with a little grit and persistence?

"You've changed, Sarabeth. You're not the person you used to be. Jane would cry to see you," Cynthia said, and she sounded really sad. "She would, she'd cry."

"Sorry," I said stupidly. It was all I could say. I went into the other room and put on my jacket again. "I'm going for a walk."

"Supper's almost ready."

"I'm not hungry." I went out. I walked. I cried. I talked to myself. And it helped a little, but that night, like so many nights now, I didn't sleep well. Partly, it was because I was remembering what Cynthia had said, that Mom would cry to see me. Yes, I knew how sorry and disappointed she would be in me. I sent her a thought, a message: I wish I could do better. I'll try.

But there was another reason I didn't sleep well. It had been this way ever since I'd moved in again. Billy mostly wasn't here weeknights, so I had the couch to myself. Not a "room" anymore, but that shouldn't have made a difference. Shouldn't have, but did. No matter how often I told myself a bed was a bed was a bed, I couldn't get used to sleeping in the middle of the room.

It seemed public, exposed, unprotected, like sleeping in the middle of a sidewalk or under bright lights in a bus station.

So many nights, I just huddled and slept for a few hours, then woke, then drifted into fitful sleep again. And somehow, sleeping so poorly, I missed Tobias terribly, missed his weight on my belly, his eyes opening in sync with mine. I was sure that if he were here with me, I wouldn't feel so exposed or so cold all the time. Cold, even though the weather had turned so much warmer.

29

≈

James and I had agreed to wait for each other outside the triplex in the mall. He was there first. The long, skinny guy wearing a dark jacket, preppy khaki pants, a scarf around his neck, and a squashed little hat on his head.

"Your hat is stupid," I said. That was my greeting, not even hello. I didn't have manners anymore. Without Mom around, maybe I'd never do anything right again. "Sorry," I added.

James gave me a mocking look from his height. "Jealous? It's called a porkpie. It was my grandpa's. He was a musician; he played guitar at clubs. He always wore this hat; it was his signature."

"Cool," I said. That sounded better, more like a normal girl having a normal time with a normal boy.

Although James insisted that neither of us really fit the definition of "normal."

We bought tickets and went up about six flights of stairs to the theater. There was still half an hour before the movie came on, so we lounged in the hall and ate Gummi Bears and talked. We had decided that other people could "go together," but we would do things our own way. We would continue to be friends. Yet, sometimes, we danced around the theme of romance, telling each other stories about the people who had ensnared, enslaved, captured, and broken our hearts when we were younger.

Now he was telling me about LaShandra, who he loved when he was eleven years old. "She was a dancer, a year older than me. I thought about her all the time—night, morning, all the time. You know what I'm saying?"

"I do. I know about obsessing on a person."

"Got it," he said, snapping his fingers. I'd told him about my crush last year on a boy named Mark, and how it had led me to name a pillow after Mark, to kiss the pillow passionately, and then to lie to my friends that Mark had kissed me. James liked that story so much, he had made me repeat it to him.

"But I'm jealous of LaShandra," I said. "Great name, talented, plus a year older than you, instead of a year younger."

"Don't forget, she was beautiful, too," he said.

"Was?" I asked, a little desperately.

"Is," he said. "I see her around now and then."

Did he know he was causing me heartache? But it was my fault. Friends weren't supposed to be jealous. Friends weren't supposed to flirt, and that's what I'd been doing.

We found seats in back of the theater. When the movie came on, I tried to stay focused, to follow the story. It was about four men who'd been friends until they stole a ton of money and got suspicious of one another. There was a lot of shouting and shooting and cars bursting into flames.

I was in a movie with James, a normal girl, doing a normal thing.

Afterward, in the food court downstairs, we got sodas and pizza and found a table. We talked about the movie and agreed it was 40 percent noise, 40 percent special effects, and 20 percent story. "Not quite enough for me," James said.

"Me, either." Even if I hadn't agreed with him, which I did, I would have agreed with him. At that moment, if he'd said fried octopus was the greatest food in the world, I would have agreed. His leg was against mine under the table. He had long legs—they had to go somewhere, but still, it was nice . . . so nice.

Later, we walked around outside the mall, and I started talking about Mom again. I got started, and I couldn't stop. Then I was sorry for James, sorry that he was with me. Dull white girl who rambled on about her mother. "Apologies for being so dull," I said.

"Oh, you are dull, very dull. That's why I'm hanging with you." He tugged my hair, and I liked that as much as his leg against mine. Then he did the best thing. He put his grandpa's porkpie hat on my head and let me wear it for a long time.

"I don't have anything from my grandfathers," I said. "Not from either one of them. I hardly even know their first names."

"Some kind of sorry people," James said.

"Very sorry people, and it's very okay with me that I don't know them. I don't care if I ever do."

"That's a sorry thing to say," he reproached me. "And I don't believe you. You care."

"No." I looked up at him. "No, I don't, James."

"Yes. Yes, you do, Sarabeth." He pushed the hat down over my eyes. Then we got into it, like two little kids. "No, I don't." ... "Yes, you do." ... "No, I don't." Back and forth like that, each of us stubborn, refusing to quit.

"You're wrong, James!"

"I'm right, Sarabeth!"

He grabbed my hand and stopped me in the middle of the street. "I'm looking at you. You can't see yourself, but if you could—if you saw your face when you talk about these folks, you'd know you're not happy about them. And I'll tell you something else—if they're so stupid, you don't have to be the same way. You should go and meet them. Don't wait on them. Do it yourself."

"Never," I said, hoping he wouldn't take away his hand, which was wrapped around mine, and which I was pretending I didn't notice. "I'll never do it."

"They're your family," he said. We kept walking, and he was still holding my hand. "You can't ignore your family forever."

"I can't? After how they treated my mom, I don't even call them family."

"They're probably good people, even if they

did do some bad stuff," he argued.

"Hello? I don't think so."

"Maybe what they did wasn't that bad, either, just—"

"Just *what*?" I said, withdrawing my hand.

"Misguided. That's what my mother calls it when people make mistakes. Misguided. Missile gone wrong. And she says you have to allow for that and give everyone the chance to get into a right path again."

"Oh, James!"

Now I didn't want to look at him or talk to him, or even be next to him. I wanted to get away from this awful conversation, this, yes, misguided attempt to make me think well of people who had treated my mother like dirt. I walked faster. I wanted to run. But he stayed with me—of course, his long legs! I couldn't outwalk him, and he kept up the "misguided" talk, reminding me of the saying, That was then; this is now.

"Yes, this is now. And now, especially now, I don't care if they were misguided, mistaken, or miss anything. They don't miss me, James! They didn't care about me or my mom. They never did, and they never will. And here's something else,

James. Chew on this! Why would they even want to see me? I was the cause of all the trouble between them and my parents."

"What if I told you that knowing them could change your life?"

"I'd tell you that, smart and brilliant and clever as you are, you still don't know what you're talking about. And I wouldn't believe you anyway, so let's just drop the subject."

We became peaceful again, but I resolved never to talk about Mom and her family and Hinchville again to anyone. I hoped never to even hear that name, Hinchville, again.

30

"**Y**ou're really thinking of going to Hinch-ville?" Grant said, and they all looked at me, waiting for my answer.

How had this happened? After my passionate vow to ban the topic of Mom and Hinchville, I'd kept my promise three entire days. And now, sitting at our table in the cafeteria, I'd not only spilled the whole conversation I'd had with James but I'd heard myself blurting out that maybe I would go to Hinchville and check out those people.

"Are you serious, Sarabeth?" Asa asked.

"No. Forget I said that. It was just a stupid thought."

"My advice is, keep it that way, as a thought, stupid or otherwise." Grant set her sandwich down and wiped her mouth carefully. "Why dig up the past?"

Asa nodded. "That could be so depressing for you. You're just getting to feel better—"

"Hold it," Jennifer said. "I don't agree. I can

see Silver going there. It would be cool." She bounced in her seat. "She could find out who she came from, her heritage, all that genealogy and roots stuff."

"I'm not going to do it, Jennifer," I said. "Even if Mom's people were still there and even if I could find them, what would be the point? What would I say to them? 'Hi, I'm Sarabeth. You slammed the door on my mom, you ignored me my whole life, and you're a bunch of creeps. Good-bye'?"

Patty hadn't said a word yet. "Sarabeth," she said. "Just go back to what James said, okay? When he was making his point about—"

"And speaking of who, or is it whom," Jennifer broke in, "there is the darling boy, himself."

She pointed. Grant pushed her hand down, but we all turned and looked. James had just gotten up from a table at the other end of the cafeteria and was walking toward the door.

"He really is adorable," Grant said, which was so unlike her that we all burst out laughing.

Jennifer nudged my leg under the table. "Okay if we drool over your *friend*, Silver?" She found it hard to believe that what James and I had was a friendship and not romance. "If he was my friend, I'd be all over him," she said. "Gaawd!" She stood up, as if she was going to take off after him.

"Jennifer!" I yanked her down.

"*As* I was saying," Patty said. "James's point was that you should know your family, good or bad. Good and bad, actually. Am I right?"

"Yes."

"And I agree with James. It doesn't do any good to bury your head in the sand and pretend people don't exist, just because in the past they——"

"Is that what you think my mom was doing?" I said. "Burying her head in the sand?"

"No, that's not what I said. Sarabeth! Don't give me that terrible look. You know that's not what I meant."

"My mom did what she thought was right." I gripped the table. "Those people hurt her. They hurt her as bad as you can hurt someone. She wasn't burying her head in the sand all these years, Patty——"

"I know, Sarabeth. It's okay. Slow down. I'm not——"

"You think I'm proud of them, proud of

being related? I don't want them as my relatives; I don't claim them. Maybe for about five seconds, my brain got twisted and I thought James was right, and maybe for about another five seconds I thought about going there, and maybe—"

"Shh, shhh, shhh." Patty put her hand on my arm. "I would never say a word against your mom, Sarabeth. When I said 'bury your head in the sand,' I wasn't even thinking about your mom. I was thinking about, you know, about my uncle," she said tightly. "Thinking how right James is, even though it's such a hard thing. Because you know it's no use for me to deny he's my uncle. He is, and he did what he did, and . . ." She crumpled her lunch bag and shoved it to one side.

"I'm sorry, Patty," I said.

After a moment, she said, "He did bad things, and it's okay for me to acknowledge that. I mean, it's part of my life, and I have to deal with it."

A silence fell. We were all remembering what had happened to Patty last year. At that time, I was sure I would never forget anything about it, that it would be burned into my mind forever, and that not a day would pass without my remembering. But now, sometimes, weeks passed without Patty's uncle even appearing on my mental radar. Was that the way it was going to be with other people and Mom? After a while, nobody would remember her, except me?

31

❦

"Your social worker called me," Cynthia said a few days later. "I always forget his name. He called this morning, when you were at school."

"Travisino." I opened the refrigerator and took out the carton of OJ.

"Mr. Travisino, right." Cynthia took a pack of cigarettes off the top of the refrigerator. "Well . . . " She lit up. "He said a caseworker was coming to look us over. Look at the living situation."

"Okay." I drank down the juice in one long, thirsty gulp.

"Sarabeth, I don't think you heard me. I'm worried. This is serious stuff. This person coming here will be reassessing everything. That's what your guy, Mr. Travisino, said. She will be reassessing everything."

"My guy, Mr. Travisino?" I laughed. "He's not my guy. He's not my anything."

"God, Sarabeth, that laugh of yours. You

sound so cynical. It hurts me to see you this way, so hard."

"Sorry." I went to the sink and started washing the dishes that had piled up. Hard? Was that me, now? Could be. Cynthia probably knew me as well as anyone. "Don't worry, anyway," I said. "What can she do?"

"It's not me I'm worried about," Cynthia said. "It's you."

"You don't have to worry about me." I put a dish in the drainer. "I'm okay."

"I know, I know. You're okay. You're fine. Iron woman." She sighed and stubbed out her cigarette in a saucer. "Let me just get Darren, and we'll talk about Mr. Travisino's call."

When she came back, she was carrying Darren in her arms, a posture that always reminded me hurtfully of the day I'd gone over the edge. It still scared me to think of what might have happened. I'd never told a soul about it, not Patty or Grant or James. No one.

"Hello, little man." I leaned over and kissed the top of Darren's head. He was still sleepy, rubbing his eyes. "You want me to hold him, Cynthia?"

"Sure. Go to Sarabeth, sweetie."

I held out my arms, but Darren shook his head, smiling slyly. "Come on, Darren," I coaxed. "Come to Sarabeth." But he shook his head and buried his face against his mother's shoulder.

I turned back to the dishes, suddenly almost in tears. Was it possible that he knew somewhere in his baby mind how close I'd come to letting something bad happen to him? Could a little kid remember an event like that and hold it against you?

Cynthia sat down with him on her lap. "Sarabeth, what you have to know is that Mr. Whatshisname said we should be prepared for the caseworker to decide that your not having a separate room is an unsafe environment."

"Unsafe? That's silly," I said.

"I agree with you! But we're dealing with a bureaucracy, and they have their rules, and they are ruled by their rules. He said if she makes that decision, they—" She stopped and gestured to the refrigerator. "Give me my cigarettes, will you?"

"No. I don't want you to smoke when you're holding the baby."

"Sarabeth . . ."

"No, Cynthia. You know you shouldn't." This was one thing, at least, that I could take a firm stand on, one way of making up to Darren for that awful, crazed day.

"Remember that they bent the rules for you? Well, things have changed in that department; there's a new supervisor. Darren, ouch! That hurts Mommy."

He was standing upright in Cynthia's lap, grabbing at her face and hair with his powerful little fingers.

"I always promised Jane that if anything happened to her, I would be the one. I'd be there. I'd take care of you. I promised her, and now it's all— it's all so messed up," she said, peeling Darren's hands off her cheeks.

I went to the sink and turned on the cold water. "Don't worry about it," I said automatically. I let the water run, then filled a glass and drank.

"I am worrying about it! Maybe it's stupid of us to keep trying to save for a house and meanwhile living like this. If only we could buy a house for the three of us, even a small house, it would be so much better. You and Darren could have a room together and—"

My stomach lurched, as if I was going to be sick. "Me and Darren? I don't think so. You just said 'the three of us.' I don't see me in that picture."

"I didn't say three."

"You did."

"I didn't say that!"

I ran water, filled another glass. "You just said it, Cynthia."

She made an impatient movement. "Well, even if I did, it was a slip of the tongue. Don't make a federal case out of it. I meant all of us, you and the three of us. If that caseworker says it's no good the way we've got things now, and she—"

"It isn't," I said. "It isn't good."

"What do you mean? What's wrong? You have that room to yourself almost all the time. We've turned it over to you. I'll point that out to the caseworker. I'll tell her that when you need it, you always have it. You want to take Darren, so

I can have a smoke?"

"Cynthia, you shouldn't smoke at all with him in the room."

"I know! But I need a cigarette right now. Do you know what I'm going to say? Do you know what your guy said to me? He said you might have to be placed."

"Placed?" *Placed* was what you did with a thing. You placed it on a shelf or in a box or under the bed, or if the *thing* was junk, you placed it in a garbage bag.

"Placed means—you know what it means. It means being put in a foster home," she said flatly. "Which we are, supposedly! Sarabeth, I can't bear the thought that they'll send you to live with strangers."

"Don't worry about it," I said again. "Whatever happens will happen."

"Easy for you to say not to worry! It's not your conscience keeping you up at night. What do you think, I don't care what happens to you?"

I turned around. "What difference does it make if I sleep on your couch or someone else's?"

"Please don't talk like that. I hate hearing you talk that way." She put Darren down, and he scooted off into the living room. "Maybe we just have to do it," she said. "Bite the bullet. Find another apartment, bigger place, forget buying a house."

"Don't worry about it," I said.

"Oh, stop saying that! It doesn't help anything." Her face looked puffy and fierce, her chin a sweaty, porous red, like a swollen heart that would burst at a touch.

The phone rang. "Don't answer," she said as I reached for it. "I know it's Billy."

"How can you tell?" I said. "Maybe it's for me."

"No, he's got a sixth sense about me. I bet anything he knows I'm upset. I don't want to talk to him now."

We sat and listened to the phone ring. It rang six times before it stopped. Then Cynthia started talking again about money and moving, about rent and rooms and savings, and I don't know what else. I stopped listening. It didn't matter what I said, or what I thought, or what I wanted.

No one had asked me if I wanted another home, another bed, another "mother." They hadn't asked me the first time and they wouldn't ask me this time.

32

"Where to?" the man behind the wire cage said.

"Hinchville," I said. "How much is it?"

He whirled in his seat, punched buttons on a machine, and a ticket burped out. "Eight dollars."

I pushed the fifty-dollar bill I'd taken from Cynthia's purse under the grille. The man looked at me as if he knew what I'd done. He held the bill up to the light and inspected it, front and back. He put the fifty in a drawer and pushed the ticket through the grille along with the change. Two fives and two ones. Twelve dollars.

My heart charged around in my chest. I was supposed to get forty-two dollars change. "I gave you a fifty," I said.

"Count your change," he barked at me.

"I gave you fifty dollars," I repeated.

"Count your change," he shouted.

"But I gave you fifty—"

Behind me, a man said, "You heard him.

Count your change! There're other people waiting here."

Away from the ticket window, I put my backpack on the floor, sat down on it, and looked at
the ticket. "One Way—Hinchville. Good for
Six Months from Date. Thirty-eight Dollars."
But I was sure I had heard him say eight dollars.
I was positive that was what I had heard! Or
maybe I hadn't. Maybe I'd heard what I'd wanted
to hear.

I hadn't wanted to hear that the fare would
take almost all the money I had, the same way
that I didn't really want to know that my plan
wasn't well thought out. Plan? What a dignified
expression for impulsively going to a place I'd
never been, carrying nothing except a sandwich, a
ten-dollar phone card, and Mom's address book.

This might be the stupidest thing I'd ever
done, though Patty and James wouldn't think so.
With that thought, I went to a phone booth
and called Patty. "I'm going, Patty," I said, not
even bothering with a hello. "I'm going to Hinchville. I don't have anything to lose by going there,
so I might as well. I'm in the bus station right now.

I thought you'd want to know."

"Oh, Sarabeth, yes! You're going, really? That's good. When did you decide to do it?"

"Maybe it's good," I said. "I don't know, Patty . . . "

"Sarabeth, I have a feeling about this. You're not going to be sorry."

"Maybe you're right. Maybe I won't be sorry."

"Sarabeth! You've made a decision, and it's okay, so go with it. Take care of your decision. Do you know what I mean? My therapist says, 'Own your decisions. They're yours! Don't be doing something and tearing it down at the same time.'"

"Okay," I said after a moment. "I'll try not to."

"Will you call me as soon as you get back? Or call me from Hinchville. Please! Have you got my phone number?"

"Patty," I said, "I know your number by heart."

"I know you do. I guess I just want to give you something, even if it's only a number, something to help you along. If I were with you, I'd give you a hug, a big hug for good luck."

After we hung up, I checked the schedule board again. Now that I had made this decision, I was impatient to get on the bus, but I still had almost an hour to wait.

I had awakened very early this morning, early and abruptly, as if someone had slapped my face. No, actually, it had been more like a hand reaching into my sleep, grabbing me and yanking me out, like pulling a fish out of water. I'd come awake sputtering, floundering. Then, in the same abrupt fashion, I knew that I'd been dreaming or dream-thinking about going to Hinchville.

Everyone was asleep. Quietly, I pulled on jeans, a shirt, my high-tops. I tied my fish scarf to a loop in my jeans. I made a cheese sandwich, wrapped it and put it in my backpack, and then added my toothbrush, a change of underwear, a bottle of water, and the book Mrs. Hilbert had given me. I drank a glass of OJ and wrote a note, which I left on the table under the fruit bowl.

Cynthia, I'm going to Hinchville,
to see what I can find out about
those people. Don't worry about

me. I know you hate me to say
that, but I mean it.
Love, Sarabeth.

I was ready to leave, when I saw Cynthia's
purse on the counter, and I opened it. There was
a fifty-dollar bill in her wallet. I took it out,
replaced it with a ten and a five, which was all the
money I had, and added a P.S. to my note: "I borrowed $35 from you. Don't worry about that,
either. I'll pay it back."

Now I found a seat, took out my book, and
opened it. This was my third time around with
Jane Eyre. I loved the story, but I also loved that
Jane and Mom shared the same name.

I read for a while, but I couldn't concentrate.
I was thinking about Patty and James, that they
were the ones who'd encouraged me to do this,
and I'd called her, but not him. So I went back
to the phone booth and dialed his number.

A woman answered. "Who is this?"

"Sarabeth Silver."

"James," she called, "some girl wants you."

It's his mother, I thought, and she doesn't like
me. She doesn't even know me and she doesn't

like me. Then James came on. "Hey," he said. "James Robertson here."

"Hey, James Robertson here. This is Sarabeth Silver here."

"How you doing!" He sounded happy to hear from me.

"I'm in the bus station. I'm going there. Remember, you said I should, and now I am."

"Am what? Going where?" Then he got it. "Hinchville! Wow. You're really doing it! I convinced you."

"No, you didn't, not really. You gave me the idea and you gave me reasons for doing it. And I kicked and fought—"

"You sure did."

"—but there must have been something deep in what you said. Or maybe you just gave me the way to convince myself."

We talked for a while. He got worried when he heard how little money I had. He was ready to ask his mother to drive him down to the bus station. "You should have, like, fifty or a hundred bucks with you. I can give it to you."

"No, James. No."

"Sarabeth, don't get all stiff-necked on me. It'll be a loan."

"Thank you, I really—" My voice thickened. I couldn't even tell him how much I appreciated it, how touched I was by the offer.

"Hey, it's just money," he said.

"I know. Anyway, there's no time. I have to hang up now. They're calling my bus."

"Sarabeth, wait. Are you going to be okay?"

My automatic response mechanism booted right up. "I'm fine," I began, but I stopped myself. I didn't know if I was fine. I didn't know if I was going to be okay. All I knew was that I was going to Hinchville.

33

❧

O n the bus, I sat next to a window. The
world moved by, pale, only the trees dark
and budding green. In a week, it would be day-
light saving time. Mom used to chant, "Spring
forward, fall backward." That was how she
remembered which way to turn the clock.

I read and dozed. The bus was full and, as it
sped along the highway, creaked everywhere in a
comforting sort of way. People were talking in
low voices, and they lulled me to sleep. I heard
someone saying, *You'll find out. Oooo-kay, to be con-
tinued.* And I woke up and knew I'd been dreaming about Hinchville.

I started reading again, but I didn't get far.
The only story that truly interested me right now
was the story of what I would find in Hinchville. Who would be there and where I would find
them. What I would say and what they would say
to me, and how they would explain themselves.
I told myself different versions of the story. In

one version, voices shouted, doors were slammed in my face. In another, all was quiet—no words were exchanged, no explanations given or apologies offered. They simply turned their backs on me. And in still another version, the one I liked best, people cried and begged me to tell them about Mom and said how much they had loved her and how much they regretted what they had done.

About two hours into the trip, a man got on the bus, sat down next to me, and immediately unwrapped a sandwich of salami and cheese in a hard roll and began eating it. His jaws crunched, and the odor of garlic wafted toward me, a smell that Mom would have appreciated. Even though I wasn't a major garlic lover, it made me so hungry that I took out my cheese sandwich. I'd been saving it for later, but I ate it all and regretted even the crumbs that fell on the floor.

The next time the bus stopped, the driver announced, "This is a fifteen-minute stop. Plenty of time to stretch your legs, folks. I want you all to get out and move. Don't stay sitting down here; it's not good for your circulation." He stood by the door, nodding as the bus emptied. "That's the way, folks," he said, slapping his cap against his leg. "I don't want any blood clots on my run."

The stop was at a convenience store off a road that bore a sign saying WITTLINGER FALLS, THE HOME OF RUSTY'S INCREDIBLE CORNED BEEF SANDWICHES. Everyone started crowding into the store or walking around, some people doing stretches. A dusty red car drove up, and the salami man got in. I went into the store, stood in line for the bathroom, and then stood in another line to buy a candy bar.

In those few minutes, the sun came out and, outside, trees and grass and weeds were suddenly green, shining, and sparkling. A woman standing by the door, wearing a plaid cap and a man's dark winter coat, held out a cup to each person who passed her, asking in a soft but steady voice, "Can you spare some change?"

I reached into my pocket, meaning to take out a coin, but instead I brought out a bill. Her eyes widened, and I thought, Okay, why not? I was sure that I had a single in my hand, but it was a five-dollar bill.

Quickly, her reactions faster than mine, she reached for it, took hold of it, and said, "Thank you! You're a good person. Bless you!"

"Oh, wait," I said. "I don't—"

Just then, the bus driver came out of the store. "How you doing, Sylvia? Got a place to live yet?"

"No, but it's all right there, under the bridge," the woman said.

"Well, keep your chin up. I know you do." He dropped a coin in her cup and walked across the parking lot, toward the bus.

Sylvia hadn't let go of the five-dollar bill, and now she tugged at it, not hard, not aggressively, but firmly.

I wanted to say that I needed that money, that today I probably needed it almost as much as she did. That, without it, I might be homeless and sleeping under a bridge tonight, too.

The bus driver leaned on the horn, and people started boarding.

For a moment more, Sylvia and I tugged at the bill. Then I loosened my grip. I let my fingers go limp. I let her have the five dollars.

"Bless you!" she said. "Bless you," she called after me, as I sprinted toward the bus. "Bless you, bless you!"

"You must have given our Sylvia a buck, to get blessed like that," the driver said as I got on.

"Five," I said, still not believing it.

"Five!" the driver exclaimed.

A stout man sitting behind him whistled. "Girl's got a great big heart," he said.

"Too big," the driver said. "Poor old Sylvia's never going to be satisfied with my measly quarter again."

I took my seat, my stomach thumping. I didn't know where I was going to sleep tonight or how I was going to eat or pay for anything. I smoothed out my last five-dollar bill. If Mom knew what I'd done, wouldn't she call me a fool?

No, she wouldn't.

She'd never said that about anything I'd done. And maybe she'd even have approved. Maybe she'd be like the stout man and say I had a great big heart. I wished that were true of me. I wished that I'd given Sylvia the money out of the goodness of my heart, the way Mom would have.

Whenever she had played the lottery, she'd always said if she won big, she wouldn't keep it all for herself.

I opened her address book again and, for about the fiftieth time, looked at each Hinchville name, as if I could make them reveal the secrets of these people—who they were and why they had acted so cruelly to my mother and father.

I looked out the window, whispering the names over and over. Thomas Halley. Doreen Halley. Judith Silver. Martin Silver. Netta Bishop. Elizabeth Wardly.

Thomas and Doreen were my mother's parents. Judith and Martin must be my father's. The other people, Netta Bishop and Elizabeth Wardly, these two names Mom had preserved so carefully—who were they? She must have known a lot more people, but she'd only written down these names. Maybe they had been her best friends. They would remember her. I could almost hear Elizabeth Wardly saying, Jane Halley? She was a good friend, my best friend. I loved her so much.

We passed bare fields, newly budded trees,

heaps of winter debris. We passed one crossroad after another, all with strange, haunting names. Mud Road. Dangerous Pond Road. Killfield Road. Road to Nowhere. I twisted around to read that again—Road to Nowhere. How perfect for this trip.

34

In the drugstore, the phone was on the wall in back. An old couple was waiting at the prescription counter. Two little boys with toy guns were "shooting" one another: "I dead you!" "No, I dead you!" With Mom's address book open on the little shelf below the phone, I dialed the number for Doreen and Thomas Halley.

It was a little past three o'clock, and I was in Hinchville, in Carrington's Drug Emporium on Mercer Street.

The phone was picked up. "Is that you, Chris?" a cheerful woman's voice asked.

"Uh, sorry, no. I'd like to speak to Doreen Halley," I said, and my lips went a little numb, saying this name.

"Who do you want?"

"Doreen Halley."

"What number did you want?"

I gave it to her. It was the number Mom had written in her book, but it was the wrong number.

"No, there's nobody here by that name," she said. "Sorry."

Next, I called the number for the Silvers. The phone rang twice; then a voice said, "The number you have called is no longer in service. Please consult the phone book or an operator."

The Elizabeth Wardly number was also out of service. When I borrowed a phone book from the pharmacist, there was no Thomas Halley, no Doreen Halley, no Elizabeth Wardly, no Judith Silver, and no Martin Silver listed.

This was not the way I had envisioned things happening. In fact, I had skipped right over this part of the story I'd told myself about coming here and facing these people. It had been a story, hadn't it? One in which I'd left out the possibility that nobody would be here. What would I do if there was no Netta Bishop, either?

I tried the Silvers and Elizabeth Wardly again, and again heard the voice saying, "The number you have called is no longer in service." My stomach clenching, I carefully punched in the numbers for Netta Bishop.

"Yes? Hello," someone said almost immediately. The voice was deep, and I couldn't be sure if it was a man or a woman. "Could I speak to, ah, Ms. Bishop," I said, guessing.

"There is no *Ms.* Bishop here. This is Netta Bishop speaking. *Mrs.* Bishop."

"Oh, hello, Mrs. Bishop," I said. "You don't know me, but I think you knew Jane Halley. I think you might have been a friend of hers, and I've come to Hinchville to find—"

"Who did you say you were?"

"Sorry, I didn't say. My name is Sarabeth Silver."

"I don't know any Sarabeths."

"Mrs. Bishop, did you know Jane Halley? I've come here to Hinchville to—"

"You're repeating yourself," she said, interrupting in that hoarse, almost masculine voice. "Of course I know Jane Halley. She's my niece. Now, you tell me how you know her and where she is. I have waited to hear from her for a very long time. When you see her again, I want you to give her that message, and I want you to tell her she is to call her aunt Netta at once."

I had come to Hinchville to find Mom's relatives. This was what I had wanted, and yet, hearing Netta Bishop say Mom was her niece, I froze, unable to speak. I hadn't imagined her as an aunt. I thought she'd be a best friend, someone like Grant or Patty, only a grown-up.

"Hello!" she demanded. "Are you there?"

"Yes. I'm here. I'm sorry—"

"You haven't told me how you know Jane."

"She's my mother."

"Your mother! Are you telling me you're Jane's child?"

"Yes."

"Jane's daughter," she said. Then she was silent, and I was the one who said, "Hello? Hello, Mrs. Bishop?"

"Child," she said, "come to my house at once."

"Where is it? Can I walk from Carrington's Drug Emporium?"

"Never mind that. What did you say your name was again? Sara?"

"Sarabeth," I said. "Sarabeth Silver."

"Then your father is Ben Silver?"

"Yes. Benjamin Robert Silver."

"You stay right where you are," she ordered. "I'll be there in a trice. Watch for a fat lady driving an old black Cadillac. How will I know you?"

I looked down at myself. Jeans, shirt, sneakers.

Just like a million other girls. I untied Mom's fish scarf from my belt loop. "I'll be holding a fish scarf," I said.

"A what?"

"A white scarf with yellow fish on it. And a blue address book," I added.

I stood outside the drugstore and waited, watching the people and the cars passing. It was strange and sort of exciting to think I was standing on a street where Mom had walked, looking at stores she'd probably gone into, maybe seeing people she'd known and talked to.

A black Cadillac glided down the street. It stopped, the window opened, and a woman looked me up and down. Her gaze caused me to think what a sorry sight I must be. "Sarabeth Silver?"

"Yes."

She opened the door and stuck one foot out, then the other, then seemed to shove her whole self out of the car. She was large, what Mom would have called "heavy-boned." She wore dark slacks and a starched white blouse. Her white hair was in a thick braid wound on top of her head.

She stood up, favoring one leg. I reached out my hand to help her, but she brushed it away.

"How do I know you're really Jane's daughter?" she said.

I took out my school ID and handed it to her. "All right," she said. She gave me that up-and-down look again. "Skinny bean, aren't you? Like Jane, I expect."

"Yes," I said. "Like my mother." And following her into the car, I thought that now I understood better than ever why Mom had left this town and all the coldhearted people in it behind her.

35

M y great-aunt had a little weary-looking clapboard house on River Street. The moment we walked up the steps onto the porch, the door opened, and a round-faced woman wearing jeans cried, "Hello! I've been waiting for you."

"Jeannie," Nettie Bishop said, "this is Sarabeth Silver, your cousin. Sarabeth, this is my daughter, Jeannie Bishop."

"Hello, Sarabeth," Jeannie said. "I am so glad to see you. Welcome to our house."

She threw her arms around me, taking me by surprise. She was big, like her mother, and smelled good. Roses, I thought, almost the same scent that I'd caught on Patty's mom.

"Whoa, Jeannie," my great-aunt said in her deep voice. "Let the girl breathe."

"I am so sorry!" Jeannie said, releasing me. "Did I crush you, Sarabeth, my friend? Did I squeeze too hard?"

"No, I'm fine."

"Well, that's a good thing," she said. "Do

you like my perfume smell? I slithered it all over my neck."

She dipped her head toward me, and I realized what it was about her that was different, why she said *slithered* instead of *slathered*, why her voice was so loud. She was retarded.

She took my hand and showed me through the house, talking excitedly. It was a small two-story house, almost a cottage. Jeannie had something to say about everything. When she showed me the guest room upstairs, she said, "I love this little room! Isn't it sweet?" It was furnished with a single bed, a wooden bureau, and a rag rug on the floor. "My grandmother Bishop made that rug," she said. "This is my pet favorite room."

My great-aunt came up the stairs, puffing a little. She stood in the doorway and said, "This is where your mother slept, Sarabeth, when she came over to visit and play with Jeannie, when they were little girls."

I didn't take up her remark or ask any questions. I didn't want my heart to soften to her, or to Jeannie, where it was in much more danger of doing so. But I began to hope that I could sleep in this room that night.

"Jeannie," my great-aunt said, "do you remember your cousin Jane?"

"Oh yes, I do! Janie and Jeannie," she sang out. "Two little girls love to play together!" She hugged me again. "And here is Janie's little girl! How old are you, Cousin Sarabeth, darling?"

"I'm fifteen, Jeannie."

She giggled. "I'm thirty next month, which is when I have my birthday. And I'm older than you, and that means you have to do what I say!"

"Okay," I said.

"Oh, you make me happy!" She grabbed my hand and swung it up in the air, as if we were two little girls, the way she and Mom had been. I was unable to hold off loving her one more second.

"Jeannie," her mother said. "Do you want to play a piece on the piano for Sarabeth?"

"Great idea," she said. "Mommy, you are smart!" Downstairs, she seated herself at the upright piano in the living room. "This is by that man Chopin," she said, her hands bouncing over the keys. "Some people say *choppin'*, but

I say it right. *Show pin!*"

I clapped when she was done, and my great-aunt said, "She never took lessons, but she can play anything. She hears it once, and she's got it forever." Then, as if we were those two little girls from the past, she said, "You girls come help me with supper now."

She set me to peeling carrots and Jeannie to laying the silverware on the table. Supper was a stew, and it was delicious. "You're a good cook," I said.

"Oh, I'm nothing compared to my mother," she said. "We girls, Doreen and I, picked up what we could, but our mother was a great cook. She could have been professional, except in those days, women didn't do much outside the home."

"Doreen is my grandmother," I said.

"Yes."

I waited for her to say more, but she didn't. Not then.

Afterward, she left Jeannie to clean the kitchen. "It's my special job," Jeannie said. "No one else can do it as good as I can."

Aunt Netta and I went into the living room. "Now we talk," she said. "I've been patient for three hours, but now I want to hear about Jane. Tell me how she is; tell me everything about her. How is she? And, of course, Ben, too?"

We were sitting opposite each other. She was in a soft chair, the worn arms covered with crocheted doilies, and I was in a wicker rocker.

"My mother . . . they're both dead," I said.

Aunt Netta gasped. Her face went white. "You say what, child?"

"I'm sorry. I didn't . . ." I pressed my lips together. I hadn't meant to be brutal. Too late for me to take back those words, soften them, or lead up to them. So, as plainly as possible, I told her about my father and then about Mom.

"She died back in November. She had a heart attack." As I told her the rest of it, about Mom lying in the snow in the park and then having another, fatal attack in the hospital—all things I had tried hard not to think about for months— I nearly broke.

Listening, my great-aunt put her hand over her own chest and drew in one huge breath after another. "So, my sister and my niece," she said. "Both of them, both of them."

She got up and, wiping her eyes and still

drawing in those huge breaths, she walked around the room, window to window, piano to couch, side table to wall, and back again to the windows.

Finally, she sat down again. That was when she told me that Mom's mother, her sister Doreen, the same person I'd thought of only with anger, had died the way Mom had died, young, of a heart attack. "Only, in Hinchville," Aunt Netta said, "there are plenty of people who believe that what she really died of was a broken heart over Jane."

Days later, when I wanted to describe my time in Hinchville, to say how those few days had spun my mind and heart around like a top, I didn't do too well. Trying to tell what I had found there was like trying to stuff the contents of a huge house into a small bag. Did I even remember everything? No. But that first evening I remembered vividly.

"When Jane and Ben were teenagers," Aunt Netta said, "just young kids . . . When they . . . I mean to say, when we, the adults who—when we, their family, acted so badly to them, wronged them . . ."

She had to stop. She straightened her back and looked off, as if trying to put her thoughts together. "It's time to speak the truth," she said, "although this will be hard, and you're just a child yourself. It was a different time then. I only hope you can understand. It must seem strange and very wrong to you, Sarabeth, the way we acted. Looking back, I can see it now, all the things we did and said without ever knowing there was anything wrong with them. We thought we were upholding our family's honor. Something grand like that. It was disgraceful, we thought, that your mother wasn't more than a child and she was pregnant. We were ashamed."

"She was a teenager when she had me," I said, my face heating at the thought of their shame. "Are you still ashamed? Are you ashamed of me?"

"Oh, no, child! No, no. I'm trying to explain to you. There was something else, too. Bad feelings between the families. Your father was Jewish— do you know that?"

"Mom told me. What are you saying, Aunt Netta? I'm proud of him. He was a good father; he loved me."

"I knew he would," she said. "He was a good

person; we knew that. But my sister Doreen and my brother-in-law Thomas and, truthfully, the rest of the family, we none of us liked it that Ben was of the Jewish faith. And the fact is, the Silvers, his folks, didn't like us, either. And why should they have? We were angry about Ben, we blamed him, we thought he was arrogant, and we didn't believe he would stand by Jane."

I listened then for a long time, without speaking. No wonder Mom had never told me any of this. I could hardly even take in the things she was saying about the two families, Halleys and Silvers, despising each other. Why? For no real reasons. For nothing. Because they were different religions. Because one family, the Halleys, had been in Hinchville longer than the other. Because one family, the Silvers, had professions and the other didn't. I really didn't understand how people could live by such stupid and heartless rules of life. And I almost laughed as I thought how much better they would all have been if they'd followed Mom's "Rules for Life."

"We wanted to tear those children apart," Aunt Netta was saying. "And what I've wondered so many times in the last few years is why we didn't just try to stop the wind from blowing. We would have done as well."

We were there, talking, for hours. Another thing that Aunt Netta told me was that, four years ago, after he survived a stroke, my father's father had called her. "Just to say hello, he said. Just to start doing the right thing, even if it was almost too late. So that was—good. And I was only sorry I hadn't done it first," she added.

It was after midnight when I went upstairs. My wish was granted. I slept in the bed where Mom used to sleep when she visited her aunt Netta and her cousin Jeannie. It comforted me to be there. All through the night, I knew that Mom was close by.

36

At eight o'clock the next morning, sitting across the breakfast table from my great-aunt, I heard her say, "Sarabeth. There is someone I think you ought to meet. Her name is Traci Wells."

"A cousin?" I said, because she had been telling me about my mother's cousins.

"No," Aunt Netta said in her firm way. "Your half sister."

Shortly before noon, she dropped me off downtown in front of a diner called Buzzy's Place, not far from the drugstore where I'd phoned her the day before. "Do you want me to come in with you?" she said. "I don't think it's really necessary. You'll do fine on your own. Ring me when you're ready, and I'll come around and get you. I told Traci's mother I'd drop her off, too."

I nodded and opened the car door. My aunt had told me almost nothing about Traci, except that Benjamin Silver was her father, too. That information had crashed into my mind and occupied it completely for the last few hours.

"Bye, Sarabeth, bye," Jeannie called from the backseat of the Cadillac. "Have lots of fun and smiles."

As soon as I walked into the diner, I spotted Traci. She was around my age, dark-haired, and a little plump, and in some unmistakable way she resembled me. She was sitting in a booth toward the back, flipping through a magazine. I walked toward her, and she looked up.

"Traci?" I sat down across from her and, for some reason, felt compelled to say my full name. "I'm Sarabeth Silver."

"And I'm Traci Wells," she said almost mockingly. And then, "So here you are, the mystery sister! Too bad you're a girl. I always hoped if I ever met you that you'd be a brother. I have three sisters already, and that's plenty for me. So, what do you want to know?"

Her brisk tone, her words, as if she was twice my age, and her cool, almost contemptuous glance froze me.

"Well, if you're not going to talk, I will," she

said. "I bet I know a whole lot more about you than you know about me."

"I don't know anything about you," I said.

"Pity," she said. "I know your mother's name. It's Jane. Am I right?"

"Mmmm."

"Mmmm," she mimicked. "What are you, a snob because you come from the big bad city?"

The waitress came over and, strangely, we both ordered the same thing, toasted cheese with tomato and a vanilla shake. When the waitress left, I leaned toward Traci and said, "I'm not a snob, no matter what you think. I'm just sort of in shock."

I had always believed my father was as near a saint as anyone could be and still be human. I had always believed Mom and he could not have loved anyone except each other or produced any child except me. But there was Traci. And though I was taller and skinnier, we looked like sisters. We both looked like our father.

"How did you know about me?" I said. "I mean, before today."

"Well, of course, I didn't know about the actual *you*," she said. "I didn't know your name or anything. What I know is about my father and how he ran away with your mother—"

"Well, that's wrong," I snapped. "They didn't run away. They made a decision to go where they could have a life without everyone disapproving of them."

"That's what I said, isn't it? Wooo! You're touchy. My mother told me about your parents. She waited until I was ten and I could understand stuff, and then she gave me the whole story about your mother and my bio father."

Bio father? Here was someone with whom I shared something that I shared with no other living soul on earth—my father—and all I could think was that I wished I liked her better.

She didn't notice anything. She went right on talking. Maybe we looked a little alike, but we were very different people.

"My mother said Benjie and Jane were a major love item in school, but she had the big crush on Benjie anyway. He was totally cute. Do you agree?"

"Why do you call my father Benjie?" I asked.

"Why not? That's who he is. *Your father* never did zip one for me. So when Jane and Benjie had a fight this one time——"

"Would you mind, at least, not calling my mother by her first name?"

"You want to hear this or not? Okay, like I was saying, when your mother and your father had a big fight and weren't speaking to each other and everybody knew about it, my mother sort of went after Benjie——oops, Benjamin Silver. Is that better? She figured this was her chance, and they went out together, and then things happened. You know what I mean." Suddenly looking pleased, she spread out her hands and said, "And so here I am. Ta da!"

"It could be kind of upsetting to find out about yourself like that, especially if you're just ten years old," I said. "That's not really very grown up."

"Believe it," she said. Her face suddenly turned dark red. "When my mother told me, I was really freaked for a while. I mean, here I have this dad who I think is my real dad, and he brings me up from practically day one, so my friends say he is more my real dad than anyone, and I agree, except it turns out that he's not, he's my stepdad!"

"But you're older now," I said, "so I guess it's not so upsetting?"

"I guess," she said.

"Did it take you a long time to get over it? I'm asking you because my mother died in November, and I'm still not over it. I don't think I ever will be."

"Your mother died?" Her face flamed up again. "I'm sorry your mother died. That's horrible! I'm really sorry, Sarabeth."

The waitress put down our plates, and we didn't talk for a while, just concentrated on eating our sandwiches. Traci was a nibbler. She nibbled all around the edge of her sandwich, never just bit into it, like me. But that was when I noticed that we both had the same broad, flat thumbs. I'd always been self-conscious about them, even though Mom said I inherited them from my father.

"Look," I said, and I held up my thumb.

"What?" Traci said.

I took her hand and put it next to mine.

"Cool!" she said.

When we were on our shakes, she went back

to the subject of her stepfather. "He is a great dad, and I think, no matter what, he is my real dad. Real. You know what I mean? That's what I cling to. I mean, okay, you and I have the same bio father, but, Sarabeth, Benjie can be totally yours. You don't have to worry about sharing him with me, okay? But do you think he would ever want to meet me?"

"I think he would want to meet you, if he was here," I said slowly. "If he knew about you, I really think he would want to meet you."

She smiled. "That could be kind of cool."

"Did your mom say if he knew about you when he left here? I mean, did he know your mom was pregnant with you?"

"He didn't know anything," Traci said.

"Really? Is that true?" I said, slumping with relief. "Are you sure?"

"Of course I'm sure. My mom said it was so weird—*she* didn't even know she was pregnant with me until she was six months gone. You might not believe it looking at me now, but I was a teensy baby. I weighed five pounds and not even three ounces, and she hardly gained any weight with me. She said that if Benjie had stayed around, she would have let him know about me, definitely. But, then, what did it matter? She met my dad, who she married when I was six months old and who adopted me before I was even a year old. He calls me his 'lucky girl.' I'm his oldest daughter. See what I mean about him being great?"

"You *are* a lucky girl," I said.

She tapped my hand. "I guess we can be friends after all. I didn't think so at first."

"I didn't, either."

"You didn't?" She sounded surprised.

In a little while, I went off to call Aunt Netta. When I came back, I sat down next to Traci and said, "There's one thing I haven't told you yet, Traci."

"What? More surprises? You have a twin brother?"

"Nothing like that. I wish it was. My father— I mean our father, or my father and your bio father, whatever you want to call him . . ."

"Benjie," she said, playfully.

"Okay." I nodded. "He was in an accident, years ago, and—"

"What, he's like in a wheelchair?"

"No. Worse."

"He died?" She stared at me. "I always thought that someday I would meet him. You know, later on, like when I was sixteen or something. I thought there was plenty of time."

"I know," I said. "That's the way I was with Mom. Plenty of time—" I reached for a napkin to wipe my eyes.

"Sarabeth." Traci took my hand and squeezed it. She had a powerful grip. "If I said anything mean to you, I take it back right now. Let's be sisters, okay?"

"We are sisters," I said. "We can't help it. Our father made sure of that."

"He sure did," Traci said. "Oh, wooo! Wait until Mom meets you. She'll definitely want to meet my sister."

Someone tapped on the window just then, and when we looked, there was Aunt Netta, beckoning us and then pointing to her car parked at the curb.

37

"Tell me everything," the old woman said. She had thin white hair, pale lips, and pale, pale blue eyes.

"What do you want me to tell you?" I asked, remembering that Aunt Netta had said not to talk too fast and to pitch my voice a little louder than usual. "Where do you want me to start?"

"Start with your name, of course."

She fussed with the blanket on her lap. She was in a wheelchair, and her feet resting on the metal support were bare. Small feet, nails curving and yellow, skin slightly puffy, and the big toe on her right foot leaning into the next toe, exactly like Mom's had.

"My name is Sarabeth Silver," I said, "and you're my great-grandmother."

She looked astonished, as if she hadn't heard me say the same thing not five minutes ago. "I'm your great-grandmother?"

In the other bed a tiny woman lay curled up,

sleeping, motionless. There was a TV in the room, a couple of chairs, and shelves holding little mementos. Plants lined the windowsill. Everything was cheerful. Next to my great-grandmother's bed was a small table with a box of tissues, a clock, a hairbrush, a handful of blue plastic curlers, and a stuffed red heart that said BE MY VALENTINE.

"Grandma," I said, taking her hand—it was warm and soft—"my mom was Jane Halley. Her mother was Doreen. And you're Doreen's mother, so that makes you Jane's grandmother, and my great-grandmother."

"That confuses me," she said after a moment. "Sometimes I have trouble thinking these days. It used to be different, but it's my head—it gets . . . cloudy." She pursed her lips. "Let's talk about something else."

"Is the food good here, Grandma?"

"No! *They* think it's good food. What do they know? I was a good cook; I loved to cook."

"I like to cook, too. I must have gotten that from you, Grandma. Do you think so?" I loved saying "Grandma."

She struggled to straighten herself in the wheelchair. "I made three meals a day for eighty-seven years. That's right, I started cooking for my family when I was five years old. My mama died, and there was no one else to do it. Father and three little brothers? They couldn't do it. My mama wasn't even thirty, and she had a heart attack. Just fell over in her kitchen and died. And do you know something? My daughter Doreen died the same way, only just a little bit older. It's a family thing, you see, but I missed it."

She leaned toward me. "Are you my Janie?" Her breath blew on me, warm and smelly. "Maybe you are and maybe you're not."

"Not, Grandma. I'm your Janie's daughter."

"How can that be? She's just a child herself. Where is she? Is she coming to visit me?"

"She's not . . . here today."

Aunt Netta had asked me not to say anything about Mom's dying. "Jane was one of her favorite grandchildren," she said. "She's been waiting all these years for Jane to come back. It would be a terrible blow to her to hear that Jane is gone."

My great-grandmother looked around the room, then back at me. Her eyes, tiny and red-rimmed with age, examined my face. "Why am I having trouble remembering who you are?"

"It's understandable, Grandma. You just met me today, just a little while ago. Your daughter Netta brought me here."

"Netta brought you? Well, where is she, then? I would like to see her."

"She's in the gift shop, Grandma. She'll be here in a few minutes. She wanted to give us time to get to know each other."

Again, she looked around the room, from one object to another. "Where are we?" she asked. "What is this place?"

"St. Mary's Nursing Home, Grandma. It's very nice, don't you think?"

She made a face. "Nice is as nice does. Why am I here? I'd like to go home. Who are you?"

"I'm your great-granddaughter. I came to visit you, Grandma. I'm Sarabeth Silver."

"Sarabeth Silver," she said, as if she was hearing this for the first time. "Do they call you Beth? That's what they called me. Do you know my whole name? Elizabeth Jane Daugherty Wardly. Quite a mouthful, isn't it?"

"Grandma, I was just thinking that maybe the second part of my name, Beth, is after you." How I wished that Mom had told me if this was so. "I'm Sara-beth and you're Eliza-beth."

"How did you know my name?" she asked, with that look of amazement.

"My mother had it written down in a book," I said. "Elizabeth Wardly."

"Elizabeth's a fancy name," she said with a sniff. "My mother, bless her, had fancy ideas."

"I like that name, Grandma. I'm glad it's part of my name. I think my Mom named me in honor of you."

"In honor of me," she said. "My goodness! I should get a medal. The old-age medal. How old do you think I am? Nobody ever guesses my right age."

"Seventy-five?" I said, to please her.

"Ha! They all think I'm younger. I've always looked younger. Ninety-two, that's how old I am. And I did everything for myself until I broke my darned hip and had to come here." Her eyes had cleared; the confused look had left her face. "Here is the death place," she said.

"Oh, Grandma——" I protested.

"No," she said firmly. "You come, and you don't get out. This is the place of the walking dead. Or"——she looked down at her wheelchair——"should I say the riding dead?"

We both laughed. "Grandma, I love you," I said.

"And I love you." She took my hand to her lips and kissed it. She rubbed a finger over my cheek. "Why are you crying? Did I say something to make you sad?"

"No, Grandma. These are . . . happy tears."

"Happy tears," she said in a mulling voice. "And what's making you happy, my little girl?"

"You," I said. "You're my sweet grandma. I found you, and I never thought I would. I didn't even know I was looking for you!"

"Oh, that sounds like a joke," she said. She paused. Her eyes went unfocused and her head dropped on her chest.

I sat and watched her sleep. I tucked her shawl around her and smoothed the thin white hair. I watched how her eyelids fluttered, how her breath puffed out in a little whisper, and I thought, This is my great-grandmother. It seemed like a great miracle.

38

Aunt Netta saw me off on the bus that afternoon. She had paid for the ticket and insisted that I take what she called "an emergency fund."

"Do you remember what I told you?" she said.

"You told me a lot of things."

"I mean that you are to call me if you need me. And you are to remember that we always have a place for you here."

"I'll remember."

"Promise me," she said sternly. The same thing she had said when we talked about what she called my "situation."

"Aunt Netta, I promise. And I also promise that I'll come to see you and Jeannie again."

She hugged me tightly. "I'll count on that." She took me by the shoulders and kissed each of my cheeks. "Good-bye for now," she said. "Good-bye, my darling Sarabeth."

➤ ➤ ➤

All the way home on the bus, all through those long hours, I thought of nothing but Hinchville and what I had found there.

Great-aunt Netta. Jeannie. My great-grandmother, and Traci, my half sister.

And more.

Aunt Netta had invited a slew of people to supper on my second night there, and all of them were relatives. One was a cousin named Ted Halley. He was a dentist, and his wife, who was now also my cousin, by marriage, was an accountant. They had three kids. More cousins, although I didn't meet them that night. When Aunt Netta brought up Mom's name, Ted shrugged and said, "Why bring up all that mess from the past?"

And from the glances around the table, I could tell he wasn't the only person who thought that way.

But there were also people like Richie Barnes, who fixed whatever needed to be fixed around Aunt Netta's house, and who called himself a kissing cousin. "Third or fourth or some damn thing," he said. "Jane Halley, sure, I knew her, went to school with her from first grade on. She always had the best handwriting of anyone. I remember in second grade, the rest of us would be goofing off, and she'd be sitting there, practicing her cursive."

And more.

Dozens of other people who were related to me, some living in Hinchville, like Richie Barnes and Ted Halley, but more of them in all sorts of places—Hawaii, Illinois, Florida, North Carolina, Minnesota, even Paris and London.

And more: the possibility of living with Aunt Netta in Hinchville. I was tempted. A new place. A new start. But I knew I wasn't ready to leave my school and all my friends, and Leo and Cynthia, and everything I knew. And even though Mom had grown up in Hinchville, it seemed to me that if I left the city and the state where we had lived together, I would be leaving her behind.

And more.

My Silver grandparents. Aunt Netta said that a few years ago they had moved to Asheville, North Carolina, for their health. "Judith was diagnosed with MS and Martin, I understand, has his own problems with blood pressure. Their other son, your uncle Steven, has a medical practice down there, so he looks after them."

Aunt Netta had their number and, on my last day, she called them. "Judith," she said, "this is Netta Bishop. How are you and Martin doing? . . . Oh, that's good, I'm glad to hear it. Well, we haven't talked for a while now and—yes, I'm fine; thank you for asking. Judith, I called because I have a little surprise for you. Well, not so little. I have someone here who wants to talk to you. Her name is Sarabeth. . . . Now just wait; I'm not going to answer those questions. I'll let her speak for herself."

She handed me the phone and, for the first time, I heard the voice of my father's mother. When she understood who I was, she burst into tears. "You're my granddaughter?" she said, and she repeated my name, saying "Sarabeth" as if she was tasting it, and the taste was delicious to her.

But when she asked about my father and I had to say that he was dead, that he had been dead for almost eleven years, she went silent. "Oh, my Benjie," she said, at last.

My grandfather got on the phone. "You're Benjamin's girl?" he said. "His daughter?"

"Yes, I am. . . ."

"And when are we going to see you, Sarabeth?"

"I don't know, sir."

I had never in my life called anyone sir. It popped out of my mouth, partly because that was how people talked in *Jane Eyre* and partly because I didn't know what to call my grandfather. Grandpa? Mr. Silver? Gramps?

"You'll just have to come down here," he said. "Wait a second—let me get a pad and take down your address." After he did this, he said, "Now I want to hear about my son."

"I can't tell you too much, sir—"

"Grandpa will do," he said.

"Grandpa. I was just a little girl when—"

"Whatever you can tell me, I'll listen."

I had never thought about all the years that he and my grandmother had waited to hear from my father. But hearing the pain in his voice as he spoke, not about my father but about *his son*, I was spun around hard. Very hard.

This was Mom's doing. I didn't want to believe it, but I had to, because the fact was, she had never let them know about my father's death. She had never written or called. Maybe it had been too much for her when it happened. Maybe she blamed them. There were lots of maybes, but there were also all the years since then when she hadn't done anything, either.

For the first time, I realized that none of the Hinchville people had known where Mom was, but she'd always known where they were. How easy it would have been for her to get in touch, but because of her stubborn pride, she hadn't done it. Just as she had never let her parents know where she was or tried to make up with them.

So that was also what I found in Hinchville.

But more than anything, I found a family— hearts open to me and arms that took me into their embrace.

39

❧

When I got off the bus late that evening, Pepper was waiting for me. She hurried toward me, holding out her hands, her bracelets jingling down her long, thin arms.

"Where's Cynthia?" I said.

"The baby's running a temperature; she had to take him to the doctor. It's okay, so don't worry. . . . Come on, my car's over there in the lot."

I looked around, as if I expected some great change in the trees or the buildings, as if weeks or months, whole seasons, had passed since three days ago when I had climbed the steps into the bus that would take me to Hinchville.

"I have news for you," Pepper said, backing out. "Leo and I are getting married."

My knee-jerk reaction was, *No, you can't. It's Leo and Mom.* But there was no Leo and Mom. Even if Mom had lived, there wouldn't have been Leo and Mom. "Congratulations," I said.

Pepper glanced at me. "I hope it's not too hard for you. My mother remarried when I was twelve, and I remember, it was awful; it was so difficult." She slowed at the entrance to the highway, then sped into the moving stream of cars. "I wanted my own dad, but in the end, it was good. My stepfather was a good guy. He's still around," she added. "I still have a dad when I need one."

"I've never really had a dad," I said, wondering why she was telling me this. "Only for two years."

"Isn't Leo like your dad?"

"More like a brother."

"Yeah, I can see that. Fun big brother, right?"

"Sometimes . . . actually, sometimes he is like a dad." I thought of how protective he'd been of me with Dolly Krall. And how he'd always pick me up and take me anyplace I wanted to go. That was dad stuff.

"I was wondering if my marrying Leo would be kind of the same thing for you as I experienced," she said. "Only the mother thing, not the dad thing. I mean, you might feel that I'm trying to replace your mother."

I looked at her. In a way, I was still back in Hinchville, and the whole conversation seemed extremely bizarre to me.

Pepper turned off the highway and slowed down for a light. "Sarabeth, Leo and I are getting married, probably next week. I hope you come to the wedding. And, right now, we're looking for a decent-sized place to live, not like the little make-do place we have. We want two bedrooms, minimum, one for us and one for you."

"*What?*" I said.

"Oh, God, I'm not doing this very well. Sarabeth, we want you to come live with us. I mean, we really want you to do that. I mean, if you'd like that. If you'd like that, we'd like it. We'd really like it!"

She shifted gears. "Leo loves you like a father, or like a brother, whatever. He cares about you; he wants you to have a home. And I want it, too."

I looked out the window, registered the banks of muddy gravel heaped on the shoulder of the road, leftovers from the winter's plowing. Live with Leo and Pepper?

"This isn't some spur-of-the-moment rescue thing, Sarabeth, though we speeded up talking about it after Cynthia told us where you'd gone."

"She told you?"

Pepper nodded. "She called and read us your

note. Leo, he got so worried, you wouldn't believe it. Then she told us about the social worker coming to evaluate. . . . So Leo and I sat down, and we talked really seriously. Sarabeth——" She glanced over at me. "We want to be your family. Both of us want it. . . . This is something we both want. I know I'm repeating myself. I'm not a nervous type, but I guess I'm a little nervous right now."

She paused, as if waiting for an answer from me.

I licked my lips. "Oh, I . . ." I began, but then I stopped.

I was trying to absorb what she'd said and think what it would mean.

"I know you and I can be all right together," Pepper said. "I know we're not real close, and I can't be your mother. I wouldn't even presume to think of it, but I think I can be a friend, someone you can trust."

Another red light. "Where are we going now?" I said.

"To Cynthia and Billy's. Isn't that where you want to go?"

"Yes, it is. Thank you for the ride, for everything," I added belatedly.

A few minutes later, she pulled up in front of Cynthia's building. "What do you think? Will you come and live with us, Sarabeth? Will you help Leo and me make a home?"

I shuddered in a breath. A home was what I wanted, but was this the way? "Pepper," I said. "I need time."

"Of course you do," she said. "Just remember one thing, please. I'm not doing this for you. It's for all of us. I want it as much as Leo does."

"Okay," I said. And then, without knowing I was going to do it and taking us both by surprise, I reached out and hugged her.

40

Weeks after I moved in with Leo and Pepper, I had a dream about Mom. I dreamed about her a lot, but this dream was different. I saw her across the street, her hands thrust into the pockets of a jacket that I recognized was mine. She was quite far away, yet I could see the exact texture of her skin and each little fine line around her eyes. There was a tiny snake of worry between her eyebrows, and her hair hung forward on her face.

Why doesn't she comb it? I thought. I was annoyed. I wanted her to be better, to be perfect. I called out to her. "Mom." But she walked on briskly. I ran after her, anxious that she would get away. We were going past our house in Road-view, and suddenly she leaped up, leaped straight up into the air like a dancer or a skater.

At my cry of surprise, she said, "You didn't know I could do that?" She laughed at me. "Don't you trust me?" Before I could answer the question, she drew a strand of hair through her fingers and, holding it out, said, "Hon, look at this. Gray hair! Your mom's getting to be an old lady."

"Oh, you nut," I said.

At this, we both fell into a fit of helpless laughter, the kind we'd shared over things no one else would ever think were funny. We were walking arm in arm then, and she looked at me strongly, with a kind of deep recognition. She knows me, I thought; she will never forget me. And the happiness I felt was extraordinary.